THE BOY OF MY DREAMS

Dyan Sheldon says that all her writing for young adults "comes from personal experience. I just make the characters younger. I thought I would outgrow these experiences – but they keep happening." She is the author of many books for young people, including *Confessions of a Teenage Drama Queen*; *Tall, Thin and Blonde*; *Ride On, Sister Vincent*; *And Baby Makes Two* and a number of stories for younger readers. She also writes books for adults. American by birth, Dyan Sheldon lives in north London.

Books by the same author

Ride On, Sister Vincent
Tall, Thin and Blonde
Confessions of a Teenage Drama Queen
And Baby Makes Two
Undercover Angel

First published 1997 by Walker Books Ltd
87 Vauxhall Walk, London SE11 5HJ

This edition published 2001

2 4 6 8 10 9 7 5 3 1

Text © 1997 Dyan Sheldon
Cover illustration © 1997 Doron Ben-Ami

This book has been typeset in Sabon

Printed in Great Britain by
Cox & Wyman Ltd, Reading, Berkshire

British Library Cataloguing in Publication Data:
a catalogue record for this book is
available from the British Library

ISBN 0-7445-7720-9

THE BOY OF MY DREAMS

DYAN SHELDON

WALKER BOOKS
AND SUBSIDIARIES
LONDON • BOSTON • SYDNEY

YOU CAN'T HURRY LOVE

Mr Hunter, my English teacher, was scrawling on the blackboard while he talked.

"When you come to write your papers," he was saying, "I want you to pay particular attention to the language and what it does." *Scratch, scratch, scratch.*

Our term project was to write a paper comparing some work of literature – a fairy tale, a play, a poem, a novel, or a short story – to a contemporary film or song. Today we were discussing collective nouns and how we could use them to energize our spoken and written language.

"Collective nouns are words such as herd, flock and tribe," Mr Hunter informed us. *Scratch, scratch, scratch.* "A herd of cattle. A flock of birds. A tribe of monkeys…"

Mr Hunter had the handwriting of a chicken and the voice of an android. It wasn't what you'd call a really mesmerizing combination. I gazed out of the window. There was a boys' gym class playing football on the field. I don't really like football – watching a bunch of guys run after a ball while they try to mow one another down is not my idea of a thrilling time – but I found myself watching them anyway. They were too far away for me to make out their faces. A bunch of boys, I thought, as I watched them race across the grass. A group, a gang, a pack... They were all wearing dark blue uniforms, padded so they looked like punching bags, and white-and-blue helmets. They each had two arms, two legs, a nose, a mouth, two eyes and hair. Like a bunch, group, gang, or pack of elks, they all looked pretty much the same. But what if one of them is Him? I asked myself. What if one of them is the boy of my dreams?

One of them could have been. My aunt met her husband in high school.

On the other hand, of course, none of them might be Him. My best friend Hope's mother didn't meet Hope's father till she was in her twenties. She'd come to California for her cousin's wedding. It was the first time she'd ever been out of South America, and as far as she was concerned, it was going to be the last. It was the first time Hope's father had ever been out of South America, too. He'd come to California because America was the land of opportunity. He was one of the waiters at the reception. Their eyes met over a tray of canapés. The next thing Hope's mother knew, she was taking English classes and applying for a green card.

I sighed. Longingly. Him might be anywhere at that moment. In another town, or another state, or even another country.

Mr Hunter started talking about imaginative medieval collective nouns. "Nouns were chosen to describe the nature of the person, animal, or thing." *Scratch, scratch, scratch.* "A boast of soldiers. A skulk of thieves. A blast of hunters."

What's Him doing right now? I wondered. He wouldn't be a jock – jocks weren't really my type – but maybe he was playing football like the boys outside. You know, because they made him do it for gym. Maybe he was sitting in a boring class, wondering where I – his dream girl – was. I groaned silently. Maybe he was walking down a corridor with his arm around some other girl, not realizing she wasn't the right one for him.

"Modern collective nouns can be quite creative, too," said Mr Hunter. *Scratch, scratch, scratch.*

I didn't like to think of Him being with someone else. If Him thought he was in love with someone else, it could hold things up. Not only were my parents together for eight years before they realized they'd made a mistake, but my mother still hadn't found the man she should have married instead. I figured he'd probably given up waiting and married someone else in despair.

Mr Hunter asked for some original examples of modern creative collective nouns.

Another thought occurred to me. *What if I never meet Him?* Not only was there my mother to consider, but Miss Houlahan, my English teacher the year before, was at least forty and she lived all alone with a cat named George. I got involved in thinking about being forty and living with a cat because I never found the boy of my dreams. I imagined my fortieth birthday. Just me and my cat. I put flowers on the table. I got dressed up. I put a bow on the cat. I made a special meal for me and opened a can of tuna for him. I lit the candles on my store-bought cake. It was so vivid, I could hear the hissing sound my tears made as they fell on the tiny flames. *Psst. Psst. Psst.*

"Mike! Mike!"

I glanced to my left. It wasn't the hissing of water on fire, it was the hissing of Bobby Bone. Bone had sat next to me since grade school because both our last names began with B. It had formed a bond. I could tell from his tone that something was wrong.

I looked up. Mr Hunter was glaring at me. "Do you think I could have your attention for just a few seconds, Miss Brindisi?" he inquired politely.

I decided not to risk saying anything. I nodded.

"Then perhaps you would be good enough to give the class an example of a creative collective noun." He smiled – like the wolf smiled when he asked Little Red Riding Hood where she was going.

I wasn't really sure what he meant. "Creative collective noun?" I repeated.

Mr Hunter smiled again. "Yes, Michelle. Creative collective noun. Would you be so kind as to give the class an example of one?"

"Try a murder of motorcycles," whispered Bone.

"Without any help from Mr Bone," boomed Mr Hunter. He pointed out of the window. "You seem very taken with those young men playing ball out there," he went on. A wave of laughter went through the room. "Perhaps you could give us a collective noun to describe them."

I didn't dare look out of the window again, so I kept my eyes on Mr Hunter. The problem was that keeping my eyes on Mr Hunter made my mind go blank. A what of boys? Not bunch, group, gang, or pack. They were descriptive but not really creative.

Mr Hunter started tapping his foot. "Well, Michelle? You've been staring at them long enough to have their image permanently imprinted on your mind. What would you call them?"

The words were out of my mouth before I could stop them. "A possibility of boys," I blurted out too loudly.

This time even Bone and Mr Hunter laughed.

"What is it with you lately, Mike, hormones?" asked Bone as we walked out of English together. He had his long black hair pulled back in a ponytail so you could see the tiny silver guitar earring in his ear.

"Oh, please," I moaned. "You watch too much educational TV. I wasn't paying attention, that's all. Hunter was putting me to sleep."

Bone smirked. "But you were paying attention –" his voice was smirking, too – "to that *possibility* of young manhood."

I could feel myself blush. It was one of the few times I'd ever wished I didn't have such short hair, so I could hide behind it. Since I couldn't, I gave Bone a shove. "For the hundredth time, I wasn't really looking at them. I was drifting."

Bone gave me a wink. "I told you, Mike, you don't have to worry. I'll marry you if you end up an old maid."

It was a pact we'd made last summer. If we

were both still single by the time we were thirty, we'd marry each other. When Bone was little he thought that God made people in batches. You know, all the dictator types in one batch and all the Greenpeace types in another. Then God scattered them on the earth at different times. But you could always recognize someone from your batch. Bone figured he and I were from the same batch. He said that meant we'd at least have a good time together. I was a little surprised that Bone hadn't forgotten about our pact.

"You're the one who calls Mr Hunter a walking tranquiliser," I reminded him. "You're the one who started snoring when he was reading the balcony scene from *Romeo and Juliet* to us."

"That's because Romeo and Juliet bore me even more than football," said Bone. "What a couple of dweebs." Bone laughed. "Romeo takes one look at this girl with Danger! Keep Out! stamped all over her and instantly he's in love. It's ridiculous, Mike. How can you fall in love with a total stranger? It has to be someone you know."

"Will you lower your voice?" I hissed. "Everybody's looking at us."

"Everybody always looks at us," said Bone happily. "It's because we're such a striking couple." He put his arm around my shoulder and leaned his head close to mine. "You with your witch's eyes and me with my half-breed

11

good looks."

I don't really have witch's eyes, it's just that they're large and two shades of blue. But I guess you could say that Bone has half-breed good looks. Or at least half-breed looks. People always assume that Bone must be part Indian because of his hair and his not-quite-white skin and his sharp features. Which actually is true. Only, as Bone says, "Not the Indians with the ponies, the ones with the cows."

I shook him off me. "And anyway," I said coldly, "that *is* how it happens. Love at first sight."

"You're confusing love with smallpox," said Bone. He gave me one of his long hard looks. "It must be hormones," he said mock seriously. "You've changed, Mike. You used to think Romeo and Juliet were as dumb as I do."

Secretly, I did wonder if Bone might not be right about the hormones. It was only recently that I couldn't stop thinking about falling in love. But I wasn't going to admit that to him. Since we were little, I'd talked to Bone about anything and everything, but lately, for some reason, it made me uncomfortable to talk to him about things like love. Especially with half the school listening in. I steamed ahead of him through the door. "It's called growing up," I informed him over my shoulder. "You should try it sometime."

* * *

Hope was waiting for us in front of the building. Bone was my best friend from elementary school, and Hope was my best friend from middle school. I was even happier to see her than I usually was. Hope agreed with me about love. We had Bone outnumbered.

"What took you guys so long?" Hope demanded. If anyone looked like a witch it was Hope, not me. Her hair was so black it almost looked blue, and her eyes were so brown they looked black. "I've been waiting for ages."

I rolled my eyes. "Bone was telling me and everyone else in the school what he thinks of Romeo and Juliet."

Bone rolled his eyes. "And Mike was explaining love to me," said Bone. "Apparently it's not something that grows, like a plant, it's more like being hit by a stray bullet."

Hope put her arm through mine. "Don't you two ever get tired of arguing?" She laughed. "You're nearly as bad as my parents."

I put my arm through Bone's. "I wouldn't argue if he weren't wrong."

"And I wouldn't argue if hormones hadn't taken control of Mike's brain," said Bone as we started to walk.

Hope pretended to groan. "I hope you two aren't planning to keep this up all night. I've had a long week. I want to relax."

It was Friday, double-feature night. Every Friday since we became best friends, Hope and I had spent the night with each other, one week at her house, the next at mine. Ever since the three of us started hanging out together at the beginning of the year, Bone often joined us for the movies. Having Bone around meant that until he left we couldn't get really comfortable – you know, pull out the couch and get into our pyjamas; and you had to be pretty quick if you wanted more than two potato chips – but otherwise it wasn't that different from when it was just Hope and me. If anything, we laughed even more with Bone. Friday was the best night of the week.

"Feel free to be as sappy and sentimental as you want tonight," said Bone. "I can't make it. I have practice." Even though he was still too young to get any real gigs, Bone had his own band. He made them rehearse at least once a week so they'd be ready when the time came.

Hope looked over at him. "Maybe if you didn't play the blues all the time, you would-n't have such a negative attitude about love," she teased.

"And maybe if you *did* play the blues all the time you could talk some sense into Mike." He gave her a smile. "Instead of feeding her delusions."

*　　*　　*

As soon as Bone left us, Hope and I started talking about Him again. It was one of our favourite conversational topics.

"Looks don't matter," said Hope as we walked towards the shopping centre to get our snacks and videos. "I don't care what he looks like as long as he has a good sense of humour."

I wasn't so sure about looks not being important. I mean, Him didn't have to look like a movie star, but he did have to be special. Him had to have a certain style. Him had to have sex appeal.

"A sense of humour is important," I agreed. "But he can't be fat. That's the one thing. He can be covered with freckles, but he can't be fat. I don't think fat is attractive. And besides, fat people are prone to heart disease, high blood pressure, and diabetes. I don't want Him tragically dropping dead on me on our honeymoon."

Hope squinched up her face. She had this way of squinching up her face that made her look a little like a gecko getting ready to pounce. It meant she was thinking. "I don't know about the freckles," she said, slowly shaking her head. "I'm not sure I could fall in love with someone who looks like Howdy Doody. I couldn't take him seriously."

A couple of boys were leaning against an old car at the curb. I gave them a quick glance, just to make sure neither of them was Him. Neither of them was. The thin one only came up to the chubby boy's shoulder.

"Actually," I went on, "maybe it'd be better if he were tall or at least regular. I wouldn't want people to think I was madly in love with some little kid."

We turned right.

"Of course, I wouldn't mind if he were pass-out-and-cry-for-mercy gorgeous," said Hope. "But it isn't necessary. It's his soul that counts."

I couldn't have agreed more. Soul was the most important thing. Soul would be what gave Him his style. Soul would be what made Him special. Him had to be deep, passionate, and adventurous. Him had to be a leader; an innovator. Him had to be bold and fearless. Him had to have a lot of soul.

I took a chocolate bar out of my pocket and handed her half. "Him has to be sensitive and kind, but strong at the same time," I listed.

"And have a wide range of interests," put in Hope. "You know, a sort of Renaissance man."

I nodded. "Like da Vinci." Leonardo da Vinci was one of my favourite people. He'd been deep, passionate, and adventurous. He'd been a leader and an innovator. He'd been like two hundred people packed into one.

We stopped at the corner. There were three boys coming out of the ice-cream store. I glanced over. They all looked pretty much the same, from their jeans and sneakers and baseball caps to the sundaes they were trying to balance on their heads. Him wasn't with them.

Hope gazed up at the traffic light. "I wonder how we'll meet..." she said dreamily.

I wasn't the only girl who spent a lot of time wondering how she'd meet Him.

"I kind of think it'll happen for me through music," Hope went on. Hope had just been made first violin in the county junior orchestra. Even though Bone couldn't convince her to take up the country fiddle, Bone said she was a natural. Hope touched her heart. Talking about love always made her dramatic. "You know, drawn together by a common passion." She frowned. "Only I don't know if he should be a violinist, too. Maybe a pianist, or a cellist... There's something very romantic about the cello. I can imagine us playing duets..."

"That's the trouble when you're into herpetology instead of Mozart," I grumbled. "Not only will I have to hang out in the reptile house at the zoo if I'm going to meet a boy with the same passion as mine, but there won't be any violins playing, just the cries of the geckos."

"Oh, yes," breathed Hope, back in dramatic mode. "But can't you picture the two of you feeding the snakes together? Bumping into each

17

other as you clean out the iguanas' cages?"

I clutched my heart and threw back my head. "Our eyes meeting over the Giant Toads!"

Laughing, Hope and I started across the road.

"But just think," said Hope, getting serious again. "Him might be anywhere right now. London … Colombia … Seattle…" She swung her book bag towards the traffic. "He might be in one of those cars … he might even be in Safeway right at this very minute."

"Oh, get real." I laughed. "I know you're supposed to meet Him in unlikely places, but Safeway?" The only boys in Safeway on a Friday afternoon were either under six and with their mother or they worked there, and I'd checked them all out already. None of them were Him.

"You don't know," argued Hope, marching across the parking lot. "Maybe his mom's working late or something and he has to do the shopping. Maybe he was on his way somewhere and he got hungry. You'll turn down an aisle and there he'll be, trying to find the mayonnaise."

"Just as long as he isn't trying to find the hamburger meat." I stepped in front of the supermarket door and it opened with a whoosh. "I'm not sure about spending the rest of my life with someone who isn't a vegetarian."

18

"Now who isn't being real?" demanded Hope. "You don't have to worry about little details like that. Those things aren't important when you're truly in love."

I grabbed a cart. "You're right!" I exclaimed in my most theatrical voice. "Love conquers all!" I gave the cart a rather dramatic shove forward.

Someone screamed.

Hope and I froze. And then I sighed.

Right there, dead ahead of us in Fruits and Vegetables, and more or less wedged between my cart and the tomatoes, was this guy. It was impossible, it was well outside the laws of probability, but I found myself wondering if this was Him. He wasn't drop-dead gorgeous or anything. He wasn't even really my type. He was about eighteen, blond, kind of short and very solid looking. I really like men with pony-tails – I figure it probably comes from seeing Clark Gable in *Mutiny on the Bounty* so many times – but this boy's hair was spiky. And he wasn't wearing an earring. I love earrings on men. That comes from watching Ray Milland in *Golden Earrings* half a dozen times. But there was something about him: wordly ... interesting ... intelligent ... maybe even a little wild, too. I glanced in his cart. No meat or fish.

"Oh, I'm so sorry!" I gasped. "I didn't mean— "

"What are you trying to do, kill me?" Even

though he was practically shouting, he had a beautiful voice. Deep and warm. Like Clark Gable's or maybe Harrison Ford's.

The fact that this man was already mad at me didn't mean he wasn't Him. I'd seen enough movies to know that. *It Happened One Night ... The Front Page ... Bringing Up Baby ... Desperately Seeking Susan ... Overboard ... Romancing the Stone...* You could always tell when a couple were going to fall in love at the end because they started out by arguing all the time. It's like a peacock fanning his tail feathers. It's a way of getting noticed.

His eyes met mine. I could tell just by looking at him that he had soul. Staring into his eyes like that I felt as though I already knew him. I stopped breathing.

"No," I said lamely, disengaging my cart from his body. "I mean, it was an accident."

He still looked pretty shaken, but he managed a smile. "I expect accidents on the freeway, not in the supermarket," he informed me. "Why don't you watch what you're doing? You could hurt someone fooling around like that."

I opened my mouth to say something clever – to let him know that he'd met his match, that though he hadn't realized it yet, he was terminally attracted to me – but I couldn't think of anything.

"I suppose I should be grateful you *were*

20

pushing a shopping cart and not driving a car," he muttered as he marched away.

"I guess that's not Him, is it?" whispered Hope.

"I guess not," I whispered back.

"But what if I don't ever fall in love?" I asked Hope as we crossed the shopping centre to the video store. "I'm already sixteen. Sixteen and I've never even had a serious crush on anyone." Sixteen and no one had ever had a serious crush on me, either.

"Look on the bright side," said Hope. "Juliet was already dead at fourteen."

"Yeah, but she was also married." I kicked an ice-cream stick into the gutter. "I'm sixteen and I've only been on one lousy date."

I'd been asked out a couple of times when I started high school, but never by anyone I was interested in, and now no one ever asked me out. I wasn't sure why. Hope thought it was because I hung out with Bone so much. She said everyone assumed we were a couple. I thought that was pretty funny.

"I've only been on one lousy date, too," said Hope, "but you don't see me getting in a panic about it."

Hope and I had been on the same lousy date. She'd agreed to go to the movies with Adam, the lifeguard at the local beach last summer, but when the time came she was chicken. She didn't want to go alone, she wanted us to double. Adam had a friend. "It's my very first date," she kept pleading. "You can't let me go on my very first date without you. Not with someone who's practically a stranger." I told her I'd think about it. "I'd do it for you," argued Hope. I gave in.

I got stuck with Adam's friend, Pepper. Pepper couldn't talk about anything but himself, which would have been pretty fascinating if his name had been Leonardo da Vinci. I mean, I could have listened to Leonardo talk about himself for months – his painting, his inventions, his music – but the most interesting thing Pepper had ever done was give himself a home-made tattoo that went septic. Besides that, he didn't like anything I liked, not one single thing. He didn't even like popcorn and kept pretending to gag while I ate mine.

He hummed through the entire movie. Not that that mattered so much. It was one of those thrillers you think you must have seen before because the plot's exactly like practically every other thriller you've ever seen. It wasn't like you had to concentrate or anything. I knew what was going to happen the minute the main character made his first wisecrack.

Adam thought the movie was great. Pepper didn't like the beard the actor had grown for the part. Hope got a headache. I fell asleep.

That date was one of the things that had

made me start thinking. It had suddenly occurred to me that I might spend the rest of my life on dates like that – meaningless, boring, less fun than ironing. I could see myself stuck with some android who wouldn't let me eat popcorn and shouted out, "Yo! Way to go!" every time the hero pulled out a gun, while my true love was thousands of miles away, looking at his watch as he stood in the rain, wondering why I hadn't turned up yet.

"I'm not panicking," I argued. "All I'm saying is I don't see any reason to believe that I'm ever going to meet the right person. I mean, what if he was born in the wrong century, or his father's a poor fisherman in Thailand? How am I going to meet him then?"

Hope disagreed as usual. "Of course you're going to meet the right person," she said. "Everybody falls in love at least once. There's a perfect someone for everyone."

In my heart I knew this was true, but my head wasn't totally convinced. "Come on, Hope," I protested, "be realistic. There are billions of people on this planet. The law of probability is against my ever finding that one special boy."

"Science has nothing to do with love," said Hope, "and you know it." The way she talked, you'd think her first date hadn't been as big a disaster as mine. "Fate will see that you find him. You just have to wait."

I don't like waiting. My mother said that by the time they got around to handing out patience I'd already left the room.

"But what if I don't find him?" I insisted. "Then what?"

"You will," Hope said confidently. She opened the door to Video World. "Everybody does."

I followed her in. "My mother didn't," I argued. "My mother found my father."

Hope sighed. "Oh, for Pete's sake, Mike. They were in love at the beginning, weren't they? They got married. They had you. It just didn't work out, that's all." The door shut behind us. "Destiny can be difficult," said Hope.

Instead of veering left, to Foreign Films, as she should have, Hope went straight down the middle aisle.

I hurried after her. "Where are you going? This is the wrong section."

Hope and I had a system. Every week we watched something from a different category. Except that we never watched anything from Thrillers, Kung Fu, War, Action or Horror. We weren't into junk. Hope and I were really into movies. Movies were one of the few interests we had in common. I was a vegetarian but Hope ate meat; I loved reptiles, Leonardo da Vinci, and Crazy Horse; Hope loved cats, Gregg Toland, and Che Guevara; I played

24

rock-and-roll on my stereo and Hope played Mozart on her violin. And even if we read the same book or listened to the same song, we hardly ever had the same opinion on it; but we almost always agreed on movies. Hope wanted to be a cameraman and I wanted to be a director – unless I became a herpetologist instead. We took our video viewing seriously. The week before, we'd watched two Hitchcocks. Hitchcock was our favourite.

"This week we're supposed to watch two films with subtitles," I reminded Hope.

She strode ahead past New Releases, Family and Drama. "I think you need to lighten up a little," she informed me. "And besides that, I'm going to prove that you're wrong." She stopped at Romantic Comedies.

"This won't work," I warned her. "These are movies, Hope. They don't prove anything. Tonnes of things happen in movies that never happen to me: my mother's never surprised me with my own phone; I've never won the lottery; I've never saved anyone's life; aliens have never dropped by my house for a chat."

Hope disagreed. "Art imitates life, Mike," she informed me, scanning the titles. "Don't forget that. It's not the other way around." She yanked a video from the shelf with a triumphant cry and passed it over her shoulder to me.

"Then we shouldn't be looking for stuff like

Sleepless in Seattle," I said, taking the tape from her. "We should be looking for something with a title like *Unwanted and Unloved in Northern California.*"

Hope's parents went out at eight. They were arguing. They'd been arguing since we got back with the videos. First it was because Mr Perez hadn't taken the screens down, as he'd promised. Then it was because Mrs Perez had turned all of Mr Perez's underwear blue in the wash. Then it was because Mr Perez decided that he didn't want to play cards that night, he wanted to stay home and watch the basketball game. They were still shouting about that as they got in the car. Hope's parents were always shouting at each other. Hope said it didn't mean anything. She said it was because they came from South America and had passionate natures.

As soon as their car backed into the road, we pulled out the couch, got out the food and the drinks, and switched on the set. By the time we'd gotten through two bags of chips, a bowl of dip, a quart of apple juice, quite a few chocolate chip cookies, and the two videos Hope chose – *Sleepless in Seattle* and *Moonstruck* – I was beginning to feel more optimistic. Sure, they were only movies. Sure, the things that happened in movies didn't always happen, but Hope was right. Art imitates life.

It stands to reason. If people weren't falling in love all the time, nobody would be making films or writing all those songs about it.

We stared at the TV in silence until the last credit rolled down the screen and the tape stopped. Hope hit rewind, switched off the set and collapsed on the pillows with a sigh. "You see?" she breathed. "It's kismet … destiny…"

The screen was blank now, but I could still see Cher stepping into that basement, like an angel stepping into hell. I could still see Nicolas Cage turn from the oven. I could still see their eyes meet for just a nanosecond.

"I can't believe anything that romantic will ever happen to me," I whispered.

"Of course it will happen," said Hope. "We're not talking about luck, here, Mike. We're talking about destiny."

Destiny … my mother and father met in an elevator. He'd forgotten his car keys and was racing back for them. She was early for a job. One minute either way and they would never have met – which, considering how things turned out, might have been just as well – but they did meet. He hurled himself through the doors as they were closing. She dropped her tool bag on his foot. He screamed in pain. She started apologizing. Their eyes met. Kismet again.

Hope turned off the light. "It'll happen when you're least expecting it," she said in the darkness. "That's the way love goes."

MY HEART
STOOD STILL

Saturday morning Bone and I rode our bikes up the mountain to hunt for Indian relics. Hope had gone to visit her aunt in the city overnight, and though I'd promised to go to the mall with my mother, she never got up before noon on Saturdays unless someone had a plumbing emergency and she was on time and a half.

"I feel something!" Bone shouted. "Mike! I feel something."

I looked up from where I was digging. Bone was about twenty metres away, flat on his stomach with his arm down a gopher hole.

"It's probably just a rock," I shouted back.

There were supposed to be a lot of relics in the woods. Bone and I had been hunting for them since sixth grade, but except for seeing a king snake one time, the only things we ever found were beer cans, empty cartridge shells and feathers. We both had a lot of feathers decorating our rooms.

"No!" screamed Bone. He sounded as excited as he did when he discovered a new blues guitarist. "It's not a rock, Mike. I'm sure it isn't." He grunted. "It's just that it's wedged in…"

I got slowly to my feet. "You're not just teasing me, are you?" I demanded. Bone loved to tease people – especially me.

Bone groaned. "For Pete's sake, Mike, I'm serious." He pulled out his arm and sat up. "Come over here and help me. Your hand's smaller, maybe you can get a better grip."

I started walking towards him, but slowly. "You're sure you're not just kidding?"

He gave me one of his injured looks. "I swear on the spirit of Willie McTell, Mike. I think I've really found something."

If Bone was willing to swear on Blind Willie McTell, one of his musical heroes, then he had to be telling the truth. I threw myself down beside him and slid my hand into the hole.

Bone leaned over my shoulder. "Do you feel it? Have you got it?"

"Not yet." My hand might be smaller than Bone's, but so was my arm. I was having a little trouble reaching far enough in.

"Stretch, Mike." Bone put his hands on my shoulders and pushed. "I know you can do it."

I stretched. My fingers touched something

hard. "I can feel it," I grunted. "But I can't get a grip on it."

"Yes, you can," said Bone.

He pushed some more. I stretched some more. My hand slipped over something smooth edged and hard. "I've got it," I gasped. "It feels like pottery."

Bone let go of my shoulders. "Be careful." He was almost whispering. "It could be really old."

"I am being careful," I whispered back. As gently as possible, I loosened the hard thing from the earth.

"Bring it out slowly," breathed Bone.

Very, very slowly, I pulled out my arm, Bone's find safe in my palm. The two of us sat back side by side. Finger by finger, I opened my hand.

"What is it?" asked Bone.

I stared down at the dirt-covered lump I was holding. "I'm not sure." Carefully and gently, I began to brush away the earth. "It's a bowl, Bone. Look, it's part of a bowl." It was made of red clay, and there were still the traces of a coloured design on the side.

Bone whistled. "Careful," he warned. "You don't want to cut yourself."

"It's too worn to cut me." I turned the piece of pottery over. It was incredible. It was like stepping back in time. Hundreds of years ago, someone had made this bowl with her own hands. She'd eaten out of it. She'd carried it with her whenever her tribe moved their camp. And there I was, holding it in my hand. "I can't believe it!" I said softly. "We finally found some—"

I stopped abruptly. I'm not sure whether I stopped because Bone started spluttering, or because I saw the writing on the bottom of the bowl, or because both those things happened simultaneously.

"Peru!" I shrieked. "This comes from Peru?"

Bone was rolling with laughter by now. There were tears in his eyes. "I just wanted to prove to you that you can't always go by appearances," he gasped. "You and your love at first sight."

I started hitting him. "I'm going to have to kill you for this, Robert Bone!" I screamed. "This time I really am going to have to kill you."

He grabbed my hands and pulled me down beside him. "No, you won't." He grinned. "Think how dull your life would be without me."

I didn't really want to go to the mall with my mother that afternoon, but I'd promised I'd help her pick out a dress for this wedding she was going to and I couldn't let her down. My mother found shopping pretty overwhelming.

If she went by herself she always bought the first thing she saw that didn't actually appall her, and it was usually exactly the same as the last thing she bought.

We had a little trouble starting the van. It was very temperamental. I wanted us to get a car. It hadn't bothered me when I was younger, but now it was a little embarrassing going everywhere in a temperamental old black van with Lady Plumber and my mom's name and phone number written on the side in purple. My mother said we couldn't afford a car. She said that even if we could afford one, she wouldn't buy a second vehicle. What the world needed was fewer cars, not more. No one needed more than one means of transportation. It would be like owning twenty pairs of shoes said my mother. What were you going to do, grow extra feet?

"Maybe we shouldn't go," I argued. "I mean, if we can't get it started in the parking lot—"

"We'll call John," said my mother. John was one of her best and oldest friends, as well as her mechanic. "Now just get in behind the wheel, Michelle, so we can get this over with." I hated the name Michelle. It made me feel like I should be dressed in pink and giggle a lot. The only people who called me Michelle were my grandparents and Mr Hunter – and my mother when she was annoyed with me. "I'll push, you pop the clutch." It was lucky we lived on a hill.

It was my mother's turn to choose what station we listened to while we drove. She put on classic rock. I began to enjoy the ride. First they played the Beatles, "Love Me Do", then they played the Doors, "Hello, I Love You", and then Robert Palmer, "Addicted to Love",

"So how did Marilyn meet her husband?" I asked casually.

"Her dentist sold his practice," said my mother. "Barry's her new dentist."

I imagined Marilyn forcing herself to go to the dentist for her six-month check-up and instead of having to get a root canal, falling in love. "Destiny…" I whispered.

"Molars and canines," said my mother. "He went crazy over her teeth. Marilyn has beautiful teeth."

I groaned.

My mother started talking about the wedding after that. The only reason she was going was because Marilyn had invited everyone in their pottery class and no one else could go. My mother didn't want to hurt Marilyn's feelings. Marilyn, unlike my mother, was really looking forward to the wedding. On the whole, my mother felt that weddings were a waste of time and money. She resented having to pay a small fortune for an outfit she was probably never going to wear again – and would undoubtedly regret wearing even once. She said there was never enough to eat and always too much to drink at weddings. She said she always wound up dancing with an uncle of the bride who had had too much champagne, told dirty jokes, and stepped on her feet. She said that by the end of the evening there was always someone crying in the women's room and someone else throwing up in the parking lot. The only good thing about Marilyn's wedding, according to my mother, was the fact that she didn't have to go alone. John had agreed to go with her for moral support.

"Actually," said my mother, "I think I prefer funerals to weddings. At least you know how they'll turn out in a few years' time."

I looked over at her in horror. Sometimes I couldn't believe that we were really related. "How can you be so cynical?" I demanded. "Weddings are exciting and romantic. A woman's wedding day is the most important day of her life."

Aretha Franklin started singing "It Should Have Been Me". My mother laughed. "You sound like an ad for engagement rings." Sometimes she couldn't believe we were related either. "This is Marilyn's third marriage," she went on. "How many most important days of her life do you think one woman should have?"

"So what?" I argued. "That doesn't prove anything. All it means is that she married the wrong man the first two times. Maybe this time she found Mr Right. If she finally found Mr Right—"

My mother managed to stop laughing enough to speak. "Mr who?" she hooted. "Did you say *Mr Right*?" She shook her head. "Honestly, Michelle, sometimes I really worry about you. Maybe I should have been stricter about letting you watch so much television when you were a kid."

"But what about true love?" I asked. "Don't tell me you don't believe in true love!"

This really set her off. *"True love!"* She was practically choking, she was laughing so much. "True Love is the name of a racehorse."

"No, it isn't. True love is what makes the world go around."

"Centripetal force makes the world go around," said my mother.

"I meant *our* world, not the planet." She could be really picky sometimes.

"Then, it's money," said my mother. "Not love."

"Yes, it is," I argued. "Love is—"

"Michelle, please," said my mother, rumbling up the exit ramp. "I'm too old for all that true love nonsense."

"It's not nonsense," I protested. "What about Romeo and Juliet? What about

Roxanne and Cyrano?"

"What about Sid and Nancy?" asked my mother.

I wasn't sure who Sid and Nancy were. My mother told me. They were the most famous punk couple in the world. Until Nancy's body was found with multiple stab wounds and Sid was found with the knife.

"That's not the same thing at all." I searched my mind for other dedicated lovers. "What about Heathcliff and Cathy? What about King Edward and Mrs Simpson?"

"What about Prince Charles and Princess Di?" asked my mother.

I went back to looking out of the window. I should have known better than to try to talk about love with my mother. My mother isn't a romantic, she's a single parent.

By the time my mother finally found an outfit she liked we were both so exhausted that we decided to stop on the way home for a pizza at Eddie and Charley's, our favourite pizzeria. We got on the highway and my mother started worrying about what she'd bought. Maybe she shouldn't have gotten the yellow dress, after all. Maybe it made her look as though she had jaundice. I liked the yellow. It was the same shade as the markings on a young Nile monitor. It went really well with my mother's dark hair and eyes, just as it went really well with the black body of the Nile monitor. My mother wasn't convinced. Maybe she should have gotten the pink. I vetoed the pink. The pink had reminded me of cotton candy. Then she started worrying about the shoes. After that she started worrying about the hat. Then she realized that she'd have to do something with her hair. That was how we missed the turnoff.

"I'm too tired to go back," said my mother. "We'll stop at the one in the Safeway shopping centre."

The one in the shopping centre was closed for renovation.

"Forget pizza," my mother decided as we chugged back on to the road. "Why don't we try that new place in Spoon Falls? What's it called? Chez something... I'm sure someone told me they have take-out." Spoon Falls was the next town past ours.

"I thought you said it seemed pretentious," I reminded her. Not that I was very keen on it myself. Even though I'd only seen it from the road, it looked like the kind of place where everything on the menu is either something you've never heard of or in a foreign language. And besides, I'd really had my heart set on pizza.

"I'm hungry," said my mother. "I can put up with a little pretention as long as I get fed."

The restaurant was called Chez Moi. It was

in a large blue house with a turret and a porch all along the front. My mother came to a stop near the door. It looked even more pretentious up close. There were a lot of new, expensive cars in the parking lot. If people saw us pull up, they probably thought we were there to fix a broken faucet.

"You go in and get the food," said my mother.

"Me?" I turned to look at her so she could see the anguish in my face. "I can't go in there! I'm in my old clothes." And they were filthy from spending the morning lying on the ground, reaching down gopher holes.

"I don't think they have a dress code for take-out, Mike," said my mother. "I don't want to turn the engine off if I don't have to. Just because the van started in the mall doesn't mean it'll start again."

"I can wait here and—"

"Get me whatever you're having," said my mother.

Inside, Chez Moi had been done up to look like a Parisian bistro. Some French guy was singing a love song on the CD player. I could tell it was a love song because he kept saying *amour*, and his voice was choked with emotion. The walls were half panelled in dark wood and painted the colour of a nicotine stain. There were checked cloths and candles on the tables and the waiters all wore black slacks, white shirts, and bow ties. The Chez Moi slogan was "A Taste of Paris in the Redwoods," which seemed a little hokey, if you asked me. Everybody looked at me when I came in like I'd just wandered off my spaceship. My ripped jeans and the iguana T-shirt Hope had designed and screen-printed for me for my birthday weren't quite right for Paris in the redwoods. I picked up a take-out menu from the cash register at the front and read through it while I waited for someone to come and see what I wanted. I'd been right. Everything was in a foreign language, though there were explanations in English underneath each entry. I'd managed to find cheese crêpes and garlic bread by the time someone finally spoke to me.

"Hi. Can I help you?" he asked. His voice was as rich and warm as melted chocolate. Now I suddenly knew what an ice-cream bar must feel like when it's dipped in its coating.

I looked up. Standing right in front of me was the most devastatingly gorgeous boy I'd ever seen. He was at least eighteen, tall and dark and thin. His hair wasn't long – not as long as Bone's – but he had it pulled back in a small ponytail. He was wearing the same white shirt and black slacks as the other waiters, but instead of a black bow tie, his was purple with minute silver stars. He wore a black friendship bracelet on his wrist instead of a watch and a silver lizard stud in his ear instead of a gold hoop. His eyes were so blue they reminded me of a clear summer sky. Looking at his smile was like looking at the sun.

"Hi," he said again. "Can I help you?"

There was something really special about him – something mature ... intense ... *different*... He had style. He had soul. He was one of the most sophisticated boys I'd ever seen. The guy in the supermarket had confused me for a few minutes, but this time I knew I had to be right. This was Him! With a smile like that, who else could it be? My heart ground to a halt.

"Did you want to order something to go?" His smile got brighter. I was going to faint from heatstroke.

I must have nodded because he reached for his pad. I would have given anything to be that piece of paper, touched by that hand.

"Name?"

I gazed back at him. I'd been so involved in thinking about being paper that I must have misheard him. It couldn't be true, could it? He wanted to know *my* name?

"Your last name will do," he said. "For the order."

I don't remember much about the ride home from Chez Moi. My mother was asking me all these questions about the restaurant – Was it crowded? Did the food look good? Was it as pretentious as she'd thought? – but I was answering automatically. "Um," I said, "I don't know … I guess so…" My mind was on other things. On the mathematical chances of our going there at exactly that moment in time. On the way one corner of his mouth turned up crookedly when he smiled. On Fate. Fate had taken hold of my life. Fate was guiding me toward my destiny.

I followed my mom into the kitchen. What else could it be if it wasn't Fate?

"Chicken!" screeched my mother. She was standing at the table, gazing into the aluminium baking tray in her hand. "I don't believe it, this is chicken!" Her sigh was almost a groan. "They must have given you the wrong order."

I was still standing in the doorway, thinking about Him. He'd smiled at me. Not one time, not even two or three times, but four. Twice when he asked me what I wanted. Once when I had trouble pronouncing what I wanted. And once when he handed me my order and told me to come back soon. "Come back soon," he said in that double-dip voice. I could feel his smiles on my face like phantom kisses.

"Did you hear me, Mike?" asked my mother. "We have to go back. The dope gave you the wrong order."

I didn't hear her. I mean, I knew she was

41

talking, and I knew she must be talking to me, because the only other person in the house was Leonardo, my tortoise, and he wasn't in the kitchen, but I still wasn't really listening. How could I listen to my mother when my heart was making so much noise? It wasn't standing still now, it was leaping around like a crazed frog.

I blinked. "What?"

"They gave you the wrong order," repeated my mother. She waved to the things she'd taken out of the black-and-silver Chez Moi bag. "This can't be ours. It's chicken. We'll have to go back."

We'll have to go back…

My heart did a double flip. We had to go back. I'd see Him again. And so soon that he'd have to remember me. This time he'd say hi like we already knew each other. This time he might ask me more than what I wanted to eat.

But then my heart fell flat on the ground. I couldn't go back. I'd rather die. After I'd paid for our food, I'd walked out of the restaurant, gone right, instead of left to where my mother was parked, raced around the building, and come back out the other side – in case Him was watching me. Not that he would *be* watching me, of course. I mean, why would *he* be watching *me*? But just in case. I didn't want Him to see me get into a plumber's truck. And I definitely didn't want Him to see me return in a plumber's truck. Besides, how could I tell Him he'd made a mistake? It would be better to live my whole life without ever seeing him again than to tell him my mother thought he was a dope.

My mother put down the chicken and picked up one of the other containers. She eyed it suspiciously. She gave it a sniff. "And this is some kind of seafood salad."

I didn't know what to say. I was too busy wondering which was worse, going back and humiliating myself, or never seeing Him again. It was close.

"The only thing we can eat is the garlic bread," said my mother.

Going back and humiliating myself had to be worse than never seeing him again. If I never saw him again I would at least still remember his smile and how warm it felt. If I went back, all I'd have to remember would be the hurt and hostility in his eyes when I accused him of giving me someone else's meal.

My mother stood there, the seafood salad in her hands, staring at the table and shaking her head. "How could anyone make such a stupid mistake?" she asked.

How could he? I wondered. How could Him make such a stupid mistake? You could tell just by looking at him that he was intelligent. And it wasn't as though there'd been a mob of people waiting to pick up their take-out, just me and a man in a suit. All of a sudden

I realized what that meant. It meant that he hadn't made a mistake. He must have done it on purpose. He did it on purpose so I'd have to come back. Not only had he noticed me, but he wanted to see me again! My decision was made.

"Let's go," I said, hurrying over to help her put everything back in the bag. Now that I'd decided to go, I wanted to go right away. If we waited, he might be on a break or even have finished his shift by the time we got there.

My mother held up her hand to stop me. Her eyes still on the table, she set down the salad and picked up the black paper bag with the silver writing across it. "I don't believe this," she squeaked. "It has our name on it." She ripped off the bill and studied it for a second. "Mike, this *is* our bill. It's what you ordered." She turned slowly towards me. "What were you thinking of?" she wanted to know. "Why did you order meat and fish?"

I gazed back at her. *Why?*

Because I couldn't think straight, that was why. I couldn't find my place on the menu with Him watching me, and the only French I knew were a few words I'd picked up helping Hope study for her French tests. But I didn't want Him to think I was so dumb that I couldn't even get take-out without help, so I just ordered anything that looked vaguely familiar. Something and vegetables. Some kind of salad.

Garlic bread.

"Well?" my mother insisted. "Why?"

I couldn't tell her. I couldn't say, "Because I think I fell in love with the waiter."

"I told you I didn't want to go in," I snapped back. "I told you I should be the one to stay in the car." And then I marched from the room before she could say anything else.

"You should see him," I said. "Everything about Him's perfect … his hair … his eyes … the way he dresses … his voice…"

I paused, his image floating past my eyes while a piece of lettuce dangled from my hand.

"And his smile." I sighed. "If you could just see him smile…"

I paused again, basking in the memory of Him's smile, like a lizard on a rock basking in the sun.

The lettuce I was holding started to move. I looked down. Leonardo was pulling at the leaf, trying to get it out of my hand. If I'd had Hope's aunt's phone number I would have called Hope to tell her what had happened. But I didn't, so I was telling Leonardo. Leonardo was more hungry than he was sympathetic.

"All right, all right. Let go and I'll give it to you." I hadn't trusted him with large leaves ever since he'd eaten a hole through a piece of spinach and gotten it stuck on his neck like a large, floppy collar. He'd looked really cute, but he'd sulked for days afterwards because he hated being laughed at.

"Come on, Leonardo," I coaxed. "Let me have the lettuce."

Leonardo blinked, the tortoise equivalent to no.

I started slowly stroking his head. He loved having his head stroked. "Come on, honey," I crooned. "Let me have it." Finally he closed his eyes and loosened his hold on the leaf. I pulled it free. But I couldn't stop stroking him. He looked so happy, standing on the counter with this little smile on his face. I decided to call Bone while I stroked Leonardo. I was desperate. I had to talk to someone human, even if it was just to mention Him in passing. I'd say that my mother and I had gone to the new café in Spoon Falls. It was pretty good, I'd tell Bone. The guy who served me seemed really nice...

"Yeah," I said. "I had a pretty good afternoon, too. After we went shopping we stopped at that new restaurant in Spoon Falls for take-out."

"Yeah?" said Bone. "That phony French place?"

"And guess what?" I went on. "I met this boy..."

But Bone didn't hear me. "So what was it like?" he asked. "Was the food any good?"

* * *

If neither of us had anything else to do on a Saturday night, I usually hung out with my mom. We might watch a movie or read or play backgammon while we listened to music. Sometimes we'd make brownies or chocolate-chip cookies. But not that Saturday night. I spent that Saturday night in my room by myself. I lit a candle and lay on my bed, listening to some of my blues tapes and thinking about Him. Since I didn't really know anything about him to think about, I concentrated on remembering his smile. And every time I remembered his smile, this light bubbly feeling went through me. The only time I'd ever felt anything like it before was once when I was on my bike and I hit a tree; just before I passed out.

I drifted into a half sleep. Him and I – we – were walking along a beach at night. The ocean stretched into forever on one side, the mountains rose towards the sky on the other. The sand shone in the moonlight. His arm was around me. I leaned my head against his chest, listening to each beat of his heart. I had everything I needed or wanted; I was lost in his love. "Mike," he whispered. "Mike, I never knew what happiness was till I met you." I looked into his eyes. I started to answer, "And I never knew what happiness was till I met you—" I woke up. I woke up because I couldn't finish the sentence. How could I? I didn't know his name.

By Sunday morning I was so desperate to talk to someone about what had happened that, despite her appalling lack of belief in romance, I tried my mother again. Hope was right: no matter what my mother said, she had once been in love. She must remember what it was like.

"Mom," I said. I was at the counter, cleaning out Leonardo's tank, and she was doing her accounts at the kitchen table. "Mom, did you know the minute you saw him that Dad was the one?"

She kept punching numbers into the calculator. She didn't look up. "One what?"

"You know," I said. "Him. The one. The man you were going to marry."

She still didn't look up. "No," said my mother. "All I thought was that I'd broken his foot and he was probably going to sue me, he was shouting and screaming so much."

I wasn't sure whether or not she was kidding. "But what about love at first sight?" I pushed. "Didn't you feel that, too?"

That made her look. "Love at first sight?"

"Yeah," I said brightly. "You know, love at first sight." I wasn't going to let her negative attitude defeat me. "I mean, you must've felt something towards him. You must've had a flash of passion or something…"

"Oh, sure," said my mother. "I had a flash of passion." She turned back to the calculator.

"I wished I'd dropped my tools on his head, the way he was carrying on."

"Wait'll you hear what we found," Hope was saying excitedly. "We were walking around with my aunt and we saw this restaurant called Hitchcock's. Isn't that fantastic? My dad says we can go there next time we go to the city. You, too, of course. Won't that be great? All the stuff on the walls has something to do with Hitch and everything on the menu is named after one of his movies. You know, like they have Psychoburgers and Chilli Vertigo."

"I can't wait," I said. "It sounds really excellent." I didn't stop to breathe, in case Hope decided to go through the menu some more. "And I found something, too," I rushed on, managing to sound pretty calm. "Hope, guess what. I think I found *Him*!"

Hope reacted exactly as I'd known she would. She screamed.

"What?" she shrieked. "You've got to be kidding. You met Him? You really met Him? Oh, my God, you actually met Him? Where, Mike? What's he look like? How old is he? What did you say to him? What did he say to you? Oh, my God, I can't believe this!"

"I can't believe it either!" I was screaming now, too. "I just walked into this café to get take-out for me and my mom and there he was."

Hope screeched some more. "Oh, my God! I told you, Mike. Didn't I tell you? Didn't I say it would happen when you least expected it?"

"It really was Fate, Hope. I mean, I didn't even want to go shopping yesterday. And then we were going to get pizza at Eddie and Charley's but she missed the exit. Can you believe it, Hope? How many times has my mother gone there for pizza? – but she missed the exit."

"Wow…" said Hope.

"And Chez Moi isn't the kind of place my mom and I usually go to, either. And it was out of our way. And we'd really wanted pizza. I mean, this is America, we could have found another pizza parlour if we'd tried."

"Or you could have bought a frozen pizza," put in Hope.

"Exactly. But we didn't. We went to Chez Moi. And Him was there! Like he was waiting for me."

Hope sighed. "She had to miss that turn, didn't she?" said Hope. "If she hadn't missed it you wouldn't have met Him."

"But that's not all, Hope." I had so much to tell her that I couldn't get the words out fast enough. "I didn't want to go in, but my mom made me."

"Jeez…"

"Any other night and he would probably have been busy with a table or not even there.

50

He probably works different shifts. But he was there, Hope. He was there and he smiled at me!"

Both of us were silent for a few seconds, thinking about the significance of this.

"Destiny," said Hope.

I said, "Kismet."

"Moonstruck," said Hope.

I said, *"Sleepless in Seattle."*

"Come on, Mike," said Hope. "Don't keep me in suspense. What's his name?"

HELLO, I LOVE YOU, WON'T YOU TELL ME YOUR NAME?

Hope, Bone and I always ate lunch together. We usually talked nonstop about anything and everything that came into our heads – from how they make tortilla chips to global warming – and we always fooled around and laughed a lot, but not that Monday. That Monday Hope and I talked about how I could find out Him's name, while Bone stuffed food in his face and looked bored. By the time the period was almost over we still hadn't come up with a solution.

Hope broke a cookie in half. "I know," she said. "You could call up to order something and ask for him."

Bone, having finished inhaling his lunch, sat back and smiled. "She can't ask for him," said Bone. "She doesn't know his name."

Hope sighed. "She doesn't need his name, stupid," said Hope. "All she has to do is tell whoever answers the phone that she can't remember his name and then describe him. And then they'll tell her what his name is and she can hang up." She turned to me. "You can describe him, right?"

Could I describe Him? Hadn't I described Him to her at least sixteen times since last night on the phone? Hadn't I been describing Him to myself for nearly two days now?

"You have to ask?" I screeched. "His image is imprinted on my brain."

"At least you've still got something up there," said Bone.

I gave him a dirty look. "Oh, ha-ha-ha."

Bone smiled again. He had this real sarcastic smile when he wanted. It drove teachers nuts. Mr Hunter once sent Bone to the office because of it, but when Bone told the principal he was kicked out of class for smiling, the principal sent him back. Now that same smile was driving me nuts.

"So go on," said Bone. He pointed to my salad. "If you're not eating that I'll take it." I pushed it towards him. I hadn't had much appetite since Saturday. The way I was feeling, I might never eat again. "Describe him," ordered Bone.

I described him. "He's tallish and thinnish and dark."

Bone gave me this flat stare back. "You mean he looks like me?"

Hope and I both looked at Bone. It was true. Bone was tall, and he was thin, and he was dark. But that was where any similarity ended. Bone's hair was always uncombed, he wore a ring in his nose, his eyes had these almost purple pupils that made him look kind of crazed, and his idea of making a fashion state-ment was to add an old black satin vest to the old black T-shirt and jeans he usually wore – unless he was playing with his band, when he wore an old blue-and-black flannel shirt instead of the vest.

"No," I said evenly. "He doesn't look any-thing like you."

Bone nodded to the next table. There were three seniors at the table. They were all tallish, thinnish, and dark. "You mean he looks like one of them?"

Bone hadn't said one constructive thing all through lunch. All he'd done was act like he was being tortured and eat. And now he wouldn't stop smiling in that sarcastic way. He was really starting to annoy me.

"No," I snapped. "He's not like any of them." One of them had his hair in spikes. One of them had a buzz cut. And one had lots of curls. "His hair's not really long but it isn't really short, either." I tried to remember if it was brown or black. "And it's dark. And straight." At least I remembered that. "And his eyes are the most incredible blue…" I could never forget that.

Bone laughed. "Oh, right. Well, now that you've described this young god so exactly, I'd know him anywhere."

Hope threw a wadded-up napkin at him. "Don't pay any attention to Bobby," said Hope. "He thinks it's cool to be cynical." She caught the napkin he hurled back at her with one hand.

Bone helped himself to the rest of my sandwich. "I don't see what you two are making such a big deal of," he said. "There's a simple, easy way of finding out his name." He smirked. "Foolproof, too."

Hope and I both looked at him again.

"Oh, really?" I said. "And what's that, Dr Einstein?"

Bone swallowed the last mouthful of my lunch. "Ask him."

I was supposed to go over to Bone's on Monday afternoon and watch a documentary on Komodo dragons that he'd taped for me, but instead Hope borrowed her mother's old Beetle and we drove over to Spoon Falls. All the way over I mentally rehearsed what I was going to say. I was going to order a couple of sandwiches and fries, and when he handed me the bag I was going to say, "Thanks –" pause, casual smile – "What did you say your name is?" *What did you say your name is?* I silently repeated. *What did you say your name is? What did you say your name is?*

"God, what if I freeze up like last time?" I said to Hope as we passed the sign that said You Are Now Entering Spoon Falls. Chez Moi was dead ahead of us on the right. "What if I can't speak?"

"I'll be with you," said Hope confidently. "You'll be fine."

Spoon Falls is only two blocks long. We passed the "You Are Now Leaving Spoon Falls" sign.

I glanced at myself in the mirror on the sun visor. "Are you sure I look all right?" All I could see was about half of my face. I hoped I hadn't overdone the eyeliner.

"You look terrific, Mike," Hope assured me.

"The outfit's OK? You don't think I look like the ice-cream man, do you?"

It wasn't until my last class that I realized I really might see Him again, so I'd had to go home and change while Hope picked up the car. It'd taken me ages to find something halfway decent. I wanted to look casual but sophisticated, like Him. The only thing I had that fit that description was this white suit my grandmother gave me so I'd have something to wear to the wedding if my mother ever remarried. Needless to say, I hadn't worn it yet. I figured it might appeal to someone who worked in a place like Chez Moi. Only with my luck, I wouldn't have been surprised if I got my period about two seconds before I stepped into the restaurant. There'd be blood all over the back of my skirt. He'd think I'd been shot in the bottom. "Maybe we should have tried the phone plan first, after all."

Hope rolled her eyes. "You look terrific, Mike, just calm down, will you?" She pulled into a side road and did a U-ie. "Look, we'll drive by a few times while you chill out. Deep breathe or something."

We drove through Spoon Falls and past Chez Moi four times, while I breathed deeply and Hope assured me that I'd be fine, before we finally parked in the lot across the road.

Hope turned off the engine. She looked over at me. "OK," she said. "Are you ready?"

My palms were sweating. *Hope's with you,* I reminded myself. *It'll be all right.* I nodded. "Ready."

We got out of the car. We crossed the road. There were two cars and a motor cycle parked outside Chez Moi.

Hope waved a hand at them. "At least it doesn't look too crowded," she said optimistically.

"What did you say your name is?" I muttered. "What did you say your name is? What did you say your name is?"

Hope stopped at the bottom of the stairs

that led to the front door. She squeezed my arm. "Just act normal," she whispered. "Just act like he's a regular boy. There's nothing to be nervous about."

She was wrong. There was something to be nervous about. Him wasn't a regular boy. He was different. He was special. Perfect. How could I act normal when he was around? Already my stomach was churning and my heart was going faster than a snake. I opened my mouth to say something but nothing came out.

"Pretend he's Bone," ordered Hope.

Pretend *Him* was *Bone*? Was she nuts? One time I actually *had* gotten my period when I was out with Bone. I was wearing lilac jeans. He finally noticed something was wrong when he realized that I was walking sideways to keep my back out of sight. After he stopped laughing, he gave me his jacket to wrap around my waist. Bone wasn't a boy. He was one of us.

Hope grabbed my arm again and pulled me up the steps. She stopped at the door and gave me a smile. "Ready?"

I was still rehearsing in my head what I was going to say – *Croque Monsieur and pommes frites and Monsieur en croûte and pommes frites,* which was Hope's translation of a grilled cheese sandwich and fries – and didn't answer her.

"Mike!" Hope squeezed my hand. "Are you ready? If you want to walk around the building or something—"

I pulled myself together. "No, no," I said quickly. "I'm fine." I squeezed her hand back. "I think."

Hope went in first. I took a deep breath, tripped over the top step, and followed her in. She sailed over to the cash register. I bobbed along behind her, casually trying to sniff my armpits at the same time.

"Do you see Him?" Hope whispered as we stood at the desk, pretending to read the take-out menu.

I glanced quickly around the room. "No." There were two waiters weaving through the tables with trays, but neither was Him.

Hope, as usual, lived up to her name. "He's probably in the kitchen," she said. "He'll be out in a minute."

In less than a minute, a waitress came out of the kitchen.

"Wow, she's pretty," whispered Hope.

I was still looking for Him, but I focused on the waitress for a second. She was coming over to us, already smiling. Everything about her was perfect: her skin, her hair, her face, her figure, her clothes, her make-up, her nails. She probably even had perfect feet. She was probably always being told that she should be a model. You could tell from the way she smiled that she thought so, too. The only thing I wanted to tell her was to go away. How was Him ever going to notice *me* with this girl around? Bone once told Hope that he thought I was beautiful, but that was Bone. Bone thought iguanas were beautiful. I agreed with him about iguanas, of course, but I could see that a lot of people wouldn't. And a lot of people wouldn't agree with him about me. A boy like Him would be more likely to notice the crabgrass in a garden of roses than someone like me next to a girl like that.

She stopped behind the register – perfectly. She smiled some more. "Hi!" she said. "Can I help you?"

Hope looked at me.

I stared at the waitress. I was wondering if Him had ever asked her for a date. If he had, had she said yes? If she'd said yes, had he kissed her good night?

"Can I help you?" she asked again. "Did you want to order something?"

Say something, I urged myself. Say "*Croque Monsieur and pommes frites*." Say "A cheese sandwich and a side of fries." Say *anything*. I opened my mouth. "Fried sand and a croak," I said.

I was depressed all Monday night. Hope had orchestra practice till nine, so I watched reruns with Leonardo till she got home. Leonardo's favourite was *Cheers*. Every time he heard the theme song he'd sway his little head. At a quarter after nine I took Leonardo and the phone in the kitchen into the hall closet for a little privacy and called Hope.

"I guess it's part of being in love," said Hope sympathetically. "You know what Shakespeare said... 'The course of true love never did run smooth.'"

I stretched into the opposite corner to haul Leonardo back before he got into trouble. He loved the closet, but you had to watch him or he'd eat things. My mother had lost a pair of sneakers and an umbrella that way. "I'm not exactly on the course yet," I grunted, grabbing his shell. "I'm more or less lost in the woods."

Hope was understanding. "You're overreacting," she assured me. "It's natural, of course – love makes people impatient – but you're still overreacting."

I leaned back against the coats with Leonardo on my lap. "I'm in agony," I moaned. "I can't think of anything else. I almost forgot to feed Leonardo tonight, that's the kind of state I'm in." I moaned again. "The rate things are going, the only way I'll ever find out his name is when I read it in the wedding announcements in the *Santa Clara Post*."

"Don't you worry," Hope comforted. "Love will find a way."

My mother knocked on the door three

times while we were talking. Once was to tell me that there was a film about the destruction of the Amazon on Channel 13. Once was to ask if I wanted some ice-cream. But I couldn't think about the Amazon or ice-cream. All I could think about was Him. I'd almost seen him again. I'd almost learned his name. The third time my mother knocked on the door it was to say that she'd appreciate it if I ended my conversation with Hope before the next millennium just in case there was someone in the world who wanted to talk to her.

"I've got to go," I said to Hope. "She's hassling me to get off the phone."

"Don't worry," said Hope. "It's going to be all right."

Bone asked me to go over to his house to watch the dragon video after school. I didn't really feel like it. What I really wanted to do was to try Chez Moi again. But Hope had her violin lesson on Tuesday afternoons and I couldn't face going in there again without Hope. On the other hand, if I went home I'd just end up lying on my bed, thinking about Him. I needed a distraction.

Bone got us a snack while I set up the video.

"You know," Bone said when he came back with our drinks and a bowl of chips, "I thought you were going to turn me down today."

What was he doing, reading my mind now? "Turn you down?" I asked innocently. "Why would I turn you down?"

"Why?" He fluttered his eyes. "The way you mooned all through lunch, I thought you were going to go hunting for Romeo again."

I sat back on the couch with the remote. "I wasn't mooning. Hope and I were trying to have a serious conversation, but you wouldn't let us." Which was true. Anytime Hope and I started talking together, Bone would barge in and change the subject. We'd spent about two seconds talking about Him and about an hour each on quantum mechanics, Mozart, global warming and Kurt Vonnegut.

"I thought we were having serious conversations," said Bone. He threw himself down beside me.

"Not everyone's that interested in quarks and leptons," I shot back.

"You may not remember this from your previous existence, but not everyone's that interested in waiters, either," said Bone. "I was afraid you were going to bore poor Hope to death. Couldn't you see she wanted to talk about the orchestra?"

"Hope?" I really couldn't believe him sometimes. "Hope wasn't bored. You're the one who was bored."

"Uh-uh." Bone shook his head. "I was the one who wasn't too polite to say anything."

I was about to reply to this, but he snatched the controls from my hand. "Let's not argue about it, OK, Mike?" He pressed play. "Let's just watch the tape."

Despite the bad start to the afternoon, Bone and I had our regular good time together. The dragon documentary was great. When it was over, Bone got on top of the coffee table and did a really good impersonation of a Komodo dragon sunning himself on a rock in Indonesia. It was almost as good as the one he did of Leonardo walking on his back feet when he got excited. Bone followed that up with an equally good impersonation of a Komodo dragon eating the last few chips in the bowl. He slid off the coffee table and lumbered across the living-room on all fours, sniffing the air for enemy smells. I slid off the couch, head swaying. We got so involved in re-enacting the more memorable moments of the film that we didn't even hear Bone's mother come home until she spoke.

"Does this mean you two are taking drugs?" asked Bone's mother.

We stopped the territorial dispute we were having over the armchair and looked at her.

Both of us reared back our heads and roared.

"Don't take hours, all right?" said Bone. Bone's old matt black pickup with *No Fear* written on the side in silver squealed to a stop in the rain. Even through the heavy downpour I could see its reflection in the window with the blue neon Chez Moi sign. Bone snapped off the engine. "I don't want to hang out here all afternoon. I have things to do."

"We know, we know," said Hope as she threw her weight against the door to force it open.

The only condition on which Bone would drive us to Spoon Falls after school was that we stopped talking about Him every lunch hour. Bone said it was destroying his digestion. Bone said he knew this was just a phase I was going through, like not cutting my toenails for six months, but he was praying I'd go through this one faster than that.

Hope flung herself out into the rain. "We'll be as quick as we can," she promised.

I started checking out the dining-room as soon as we walked through the door. Only a few of the tables were occupied. All of the waiters were talking together behind the bar. From what they were saying, it sounded like the shift was about to change. Him wasn't among them. That might mean he was working nights.

The waitress from Monday separated herself from the others and came over to us with a smile. "What'll it be?" She winked. "Another order of sand and frog?"

"I think we should get a piece of chocolate cake for Bone, too," said Hope.

I said, "No."

Hope and the waitress looked at me. They were both surprised.

"I didn't mean we shouldn't get Bone something," I said quickly, not meeting Hope's eyes. "I meant that we'd like a table."

The waitress picked up two menus and strode across the room.

"What, are you crazy or something?" hissed Hope as we followed her to a back corner. "We can't stay here. Bone's going to have a fit."

I hadn't planned to ask for a table. I knew Bone was waiting in the truck for us, and that patience wasn't his most outstanding quality. But Him might be arriving at any minute. And, to tell the truth, I was beginning to get a little desperate. I'd already started to worry that if much more time passed I might not recognize Him when I did see Him again. Besides, fantasizing about someone without a name was becoming a little boring. Every time I got us into a clinch where he leaned forward and whispered, "Mike, I love you," I had to stop. I couldn't very well whisper back, "And I love you, too, whatever you're called."

"We won't stay long," I assured her. I took the seat that faced the door. "Ten minutes. Fifteen, tops. Just in case Him turns up."

"Ten minutes," said Hope. "We can't leave Bone sitting in the rain for more than that."

Hope ordered an espresso and I ordered a lemonade. Ten minutes passed. Then twelve. Our waitress and one of the waiters left, but no one new came in.

Hope put down her cup. "Let's get the bill and order the cake." She sighed. "If we don't get out of here Bone's going to leave without us. I don't want to have to walk six miles home in this rain if I can help it."

"Five more minutes," I begged. "Maybe Him's on his way but the weather's held him up."

Hope watched the clock and I watched the door.

Five minutes came and five minutes went. Then six. Then seven.

Hope pushed back her chair. Just as the door started to open.

"Sit down!" I ordered. "Someone's coming in. This could be Him."

Hope dropped back in her chair as the door flew open and a slender male figure rushed into the room in a blast of wind and water.

"Well?" whispered Hope. "Is that Him?"

I couldn't answer her. Every cell in my body seemed to be exploding. My stomach was in turmoil. My heart was hysterical. It was really Him. After all these nights and days, it was Him! It really was! Thank God my hair hadn't gone all frizzy in the rain. I sat up straight. I took a deep breath. I got ready to smile. And then I realized Him was with someone. They were deep in conversation by the door.

Hope whistled softly. "He's gorgeous," she whispered. "He looks like he should be in the movies or something." And then she too finally noticed that Him wasn't alone. "Jeez," she breathed, "don't tell me *they're* friends."

"They can't be," I croaked back. They couldn't be. The person with Him didn't have any friends except me and Hope and the guys in his band. The person with Him was Bone.

Nodding and smiling, the two of them shook hands. Him headed for the door marked Office. Bone started looking around the room.

"I don't believe this!" Bone shouted the second he saw us. "I'm sitting out in the truck, freezing my butt off, and you two are in here having tea."

If I'd been capable of speech, I would have said, "Actually, what we're having is coffee and lemonade," but I wasn't capable of speech. I was paralysed by a combination of ecstasy and terror. Ecstasy because I was in the same room as Him. Terror because I couldn't decide which I was more afraid of: the possibility that Him wouldn't leave the room without seeing me, or the possibility that he would.

Hope, however, could still speak. "We were

just coming," she said. She jumped to her feet.

"Just coming?" roared Bone. The only way his voice could have been any louder was if he'd had a microphone and the sound system of a heavy metal band. "What do you mean just coming? You were supposed to get your order and leave."

I didn't move. I couldn't. Him had his hand on the knob of the door to the office. He was the only person in the place who wasn't looking at us. The office door opened.

"And what about you?" Bone yelled. "Were you just coming, too, Mike? Or have you decided to move in here?"

Him turned. He gave a quick glance at me and Hope and then he smiled at Bone. "See you around, Bobby," he called. The office door shut.

Bone glared at me. "You can probably count on it," he said sourly.

I'm not sure why, but I didn't want Bone to know that the boy he'd been talking to was *my* boy. Not yet. When the time came for Bone to know, I'd tell him. Like when Him and I were going steady. If I'd told Bone now, it would have given him that much longer to torment me. I gave Hope a nudge as we followed him out to the truck.

Hope raised one eyebrow. "What?" she mouthed.

I pointed at Bone. "Don't tell him," I mouthed back.

Hope gave me a funny look, but it wasn't because she didn't understand what I said. She nodded.

I concentrated on seeming normal even though just the thought that Bone actually knew Him to talk to had destroyed my nervous system.

"I'm really sorry," I apologized as the three of us ran through the rain. "It was totally my fault, Bone. Hope wanted to leave, but I insisted we sit down."

Bone tore open the driver's door. For the first time, I realized that he wasn't kidding, he was really mad. In all the years we'd been friends, I never remembered him getting really mad at me before.

"What were you going to do, Mike?" Bone sneered. "Leave me sitting out here till they closed? Didn't you think I'd noticed you hadn't come back?" The door banged shut.

"Of course we weren't going to leave you there," I said as I climbed in beside him. "We were just going when you came in. And anyway," I went on, "it wasn't *that* long. What about all the hours I've spent waiting for you to finish rehearsing?"

Bone decided to ignore that.

"You wouldn't want to be hanging from a tree all the time I waited for you," he mumbled.

I decided to try a little honesty. Bone usually responded well to honesty. I shrugged helplessly. "I'm sorry, Bone. We just wanted to make sure he wasn't there, that's all." I put a hand on his arm. "I'm really, really sorry."

Bone started adjusting the rear-view mirror. "All right," he said finally – and grudgingly. "I'll forgive you this time, but don't let it happen again."

"It won't," I promised. "I swear it won't."

Bone put a tape on, and we clanked and rumbled out of the parking lot.

After a few minutes, I glanced over at Hope and kicked her foot. One of the greatest things about having a best friend like Hope was that she usually knew what I was thinking without having to be told.

"So, Bobby," Hope said, all innocence, "who was that boy you were talking to?" She leaned across me and smiled at him. "I can't believe you'd be friends with someone who works in a phony place like that," she teased.

Bone grinned back. "I wouldn't," he said. "Bill Copeland isn't my friend."

Bill Copeland ... the words thundered through my head. Bill. Bill Copeland. At last I knew his name! It was like having some secret connection with him. It was like a charm. It was a magic chant. Bill, Bill, Bill, Bill.

I controlled my excitement and looked over at Bone. Casual, but curious. "Really?" I said.

71

"You seemed pretty friendly."

Bone downshifted as we came to a sharp bend. "Just because someone's smiling at you doesn't mean he's your friend," he informed me.

I raised my arms. "Thank God for the wisdom of Robert Bone. We'd all be lost without it."

Hope stepped on my foot. "Well, whose friend is he, then?" she asked.

Bone shifted up and we lurched around the curve. "Mark's."

Mark was Bone's older brother. Bone said it wasn't so much that he and Mark didn't like each other. It was more that, except for the accident of being born to the same set of parents, they had nothing in common. When he was little, Bone used to beg his parents to tell him he was adopted because he didn't want to be related to Mark.

"You must've seen him before at the house," Bone said to me as we ploughed through the rain. "He was always around."

I shook my head. "I don't remember seeing him." But I was trying to. I pictured myself in Bone's living-room, flipping through Bone's *National Geographic*s or playing some board game, and forced memories of Mark and his friends into my brain. But all I saw was a cloud of large loud boys who might stop to tease Bone, or make some joke about him or us, or "accidentally" kick the Monopoly houses across the rug, but who otherwise had nothing to do with us. I could barely remember Mark, never mind his friends. They'd all seemed the same to me. They were older. They weren't interested in us. If they did notice us, it was only to torment us. And for that reason we not only weren't interested in them, we'd actively avoided them.

"Well, he was there," said Bone.

I gave Hope another kick.

"What's he like?" she asked casually.

"I just told you," said Bone. "He's a friend of Mark's."

I groaned. "But Hope doesn't know Mark," I pointed out.

"Then, that's one advantage she has over you and me." Bone glanced over at Hope. "Think of yourself as having had a lucky escape," he told her.

"That boy didn't look that bad." Hope laughed.

"Appearances can be deceptive," said Bone. "You can't—"

I looked over to see why he'd suddenly stopped talking. Bone glanced over at me. He looked suddenly suspicious.

"Why are you two so interested in Bill Copeland?" he demanded.

"No reason," said Hope quickly. "We were just curious, that's all."

Bone snorted. "No, you're not."

We were just coming up to my road. Usually, we left Hope off first, since Bone had to pass my road again on his way home. But not today, apparently. Bone turned into my road so sharply that we all slid to the left.

"Bill Copeland's *Him*, isn't he?" asked Bone.

Neither of us answered. It wasn't exactly a question.

We bumped to a stop in front of my house. "I don't believe it," Bone said to the windshield. "Bill Copeland!" He turned to me again. "You really better get some medical advice, Mike," said Bone. "Those hormones are damaging your brain."

Hope called me as soon as she got home.

"Jeez, what a ride," said Hope. "You'd almost think Bone was jealous or something, the way he carried on. I haven't seen him this worked up since the French detonated those nuclear bombs."

"You mean he talked about *Him*?"

"Talked about Him?" Hope sighed. "As soon as you got out of the pickup he couldn't talk about anything else."

I was so excited I was practically jumping up and down. "Well, tell me," I shrieked. "Tell me every single thing he said."

"You're not going to like it," warned Hope.

"It wasn't very complimentary."

I didn't care. "Bone's just got a thing about his brother and anyone his brother likes," I told her. "What he thinks about Bill doesn't count."

According to Robert Bone, Bill Copeland was all right, if you didn't mind talking about basketball all the time.

"Didn't he tell you anything useful?" I demanded. "You know, like Bill's address or his sign?"

"Well..." Hope laughed. "I don't know what his sign is, but I did manage to get a few things out of Bone."

I sank to the floor. "Stop tormenting me," I begged. "Tell me what you found out."

Considering how quiet and polite Hope usually was, she hadn't done too badly. Bill Copeland was studying business at Santa Clara.

"Business?" I shrieked. I hadn't realized that you had to go to school to be a businessman. My mother was a businessman, since she had her own business, and she never went to school for it. She went to school to be a plumber. "What does that mean, he's studying business?"

"I'm just telling you what Bobby said," said Hope. "And that's all he said."

I calmed myself down. Business sounded OK to me. It showed he was serious. It showed he had goals. "What else did Bone say?"

Hope took a deep breath. "He said Bill used to go steady with a cheerleader."

I knew the exact tone Bone would have used when he said that. Sneering. And he wouldn't have said "cheerleader", he would have said "pom-pom shaker". Bone said you couldn't take seriously anyone whose idea of achievement was leaping in the air with a fist full of shredded paper. And I'd always agreed. In my experience, cheerleaders all looked like they did commercials for tampons or suntan oil, and they never spoke to girls like Hope or me unless they wanted to know what the homework was. But now I had to rethink that. If Bill had gone out with a cheerleader, then they must be different than I'd thought. "Used to?" I repeated. "What do you mean he used to?"

Hope sighed heavily. "I mean that he used to, that's what I mean."

"But not any more?" I persisted. This was something I had to be clear about.

"No," said Hope, sounding incredibly patient. "Not any more."

"That's not all, is it? That's not all Bone said?"

"No," said Hope. "That's not all." I could tell from her voice that she was smiling. "Bone said Bill lives somewhere between Smoke Hole Road and Jefferson Way."

"But where?" I couldn't seem to stop shrieking. "Smoke Hole Road's about a hundred miles long! Didn't you find out where?"

"No," said Hope. "I didn't." I could tell from her voice that she'd stopped smiling. "I'm sorry I'm such a bad detective, Mike. Next time you can ask him yourself."

IT GOES TO SHOW YOU NEVER CAN TELL

For the rest of the week Bone and I acted like nothing had happened. That is, we acted like Bill Copeland had never happened. I made a point of never talking about Bill Copeland when Bone was around. And Bone made a point of never bringing him up. Bone never told me what a dope he thought I was for falling for someone who liked basketball, pom-pom shakers and Bone's big brother. And I never told Bone how disappointed I was in him for turning on me at a time when I needed my real friends most. We went to classes together and ate lunch together and even finished building a new run in the backyard for Leonardo as though we lived in a Bill Copeland–free world.

Until Friday.

Friday over lunch Bone said, "So what are we watching tonight?"

Hope picked up her drink. "Subtitles."

"How about Japanese?" asked Bone. "I'm in the mood for blood and gloom."

I kept my eyes on my lunch. "I thought you had practice," I mumbled.

Bone looked at me. "That was last week." He grinned. "This week I'm all yours."

That was the trouble: I didn't want Bone to be all mine tonight. I wanted Hope to be all mine so we could talk about Bill and how we were going to spend the next day trying to find his house.

"I'm not into anything heavy," I said, still staring at my sandwich. "I was kind of thinking a musical might be nice." Bone never cared what we watched. Even if it was something he knew he wasn't going to like, he didn't care. He said it gave him a chance to prove he was right. But I was hoping he might draw the line at musicals. He had roughly the same opinion of them as he had of cheerleaders.

Unfortunately, I was wrong.

"Whatever," said Bone. "Aesthetic torture is just as good as blood and gloom."

Hope said, "Musicals?" Bone wasn't the only one who didn't like them.

I gave her a look. It was a *Just go along with me* kind of look. "Just for a change," I explained.

"For a *change*?" Not only didn't Hope understand my look, but she was giving me one

of her own. This one said, *What, are you crazy?*
"But you hate musicals, Mike. You're the only
person I know who's never seen *The Sound of
Music*."

Bone winked at her. "No, she's not."

"Well," said Hope, turning back to me, "if
neither of you likes musicals, and I don't like
musicals, why are we going to watch one?"

I could have killed her. Whose side was she
on? How could she not know that I was trying
to dump Bone, not trying to spend the night
watching people burst into song every ten minutes?

Bone looked at me, too. "Yeah, Mike.
Why?"

I stared back. What a good question.

Hope frowned. "Is there something wrong,
Mike?" She sounded concerned.

"Wrong?"

She nodded. "Yeah, you look like you're in
pain."

From wanting to murder her, I now wanted
to hug her. Hope Perez was a genius. A defi-
nite genius. She'd come up with the answer to
my problem. If I could convince them I was
sick, Bone would give up and I could hang out
with Hope without him knowing.

I lowered my voice and made my eyes
smaller. "Well, to tell you the truth," I said
slowly, "I'm not really feeling very well." I
rubbed my neck. "I think I may be coming

down with something."

Hope leaned over and put her hand on my forehead. "You don't have a fever."

"Are you sure?" I was trying so hard to look and sound like someone about to collapse with the flu that I was actually starting to feel a little sick. "I feel really hot." I rubbed my neck again. "My throat's a little sore."

Bone reached over and felt my forehead. "She's right, no fever. So it isn't smallpox or the plague."

"Maybe we better forget about tonight," said Hope reluctantly. I knew Bone could always find something else to do, but Hope counted on Fridays the same way that I did. She was torn between wanting to spend the night with me and not wanting to be responsible if I dropped dead in the middle of the movie.

Bone pressed his fingers against my neck. "Your glands aren't up," he assured me. "You'll be fine."

When I didn't answer, Hope said, "Maybe you should rest." She met my eyes. "So you're all right tomorrow," she added softly.

"Oh, no," I protested feebly. "It's Friday night."

"But if you don't feel well…"

She was disappointed. She wanted me to say I was all right really. I pushed my untouched sandwich away. "You're sure you don't mind?" I asked.

"Of course," said Hope. But she didn't say it with any conviction.

Bone gave me a look. He could tell she was disappointed, too. "Why should Hope mind?" he suddenly demanded. "She's still got me."

"Got *you*?" I was so surprised I forgot to keep my voice down.

Bone shrugged. "Sure. Just because you can't make it, doesn't mean we can't watch something by ourselves."

"Really?" Hope sounded as surprised as I was – but also a lot happier.

I was about to say that I wasn't feeling that awful after all, but Bone didn't give me the chance.

"Sure," he said. "I'll bring the snacks."

I didn't have such a great night. It was weird, being alone on a Friday. I missed Hope. I really wanted to talk to her. She was coming over first thing in the morning, but she'd promised to call me after Bone went home. Only he must have stayed pretty late because she never phoned.

All I could think about was Bill. I wrote his name on my notebooks, I wrote his name on my calendar, I even drew a heart with the initials B.C. in its centre on my arm. Then Leonardo and I sat on the floor of my room and I talked to him about love, romance and

Bill Copeland while my mother sat in the living-room, watching *The War of the Roses* to "get her in the mood" for Marilyn's wedding. I must have finally fallen asleep because I woke up at two in the morning with my head on my shoes and my arm around Leonardo. Leonardo was snoring.

By the time Leonardo and I got up, my mother was locked in the bathroom, banging around and muttering as she got ready for the wedding, so I skipped showering and went straight to breakfast.

John and Hope were in the kitchen. John had let Hope in, but she hadn't wanted to wake me, in case I still wasn't feeling well. John was making coffee. He was wearing an old pair of jeans and a faded flannel shirt. You'd think he was on his way to a baseball game. No wonder my mother had decided to go to the wedding with John. He was obviously even less romantic than she was. Hope was sitting at the table, rewrapping Marilyn's present.

"You should've seen how he did this," she said, holding up the box in its silver paper. "It looked like some kind of wreckage."

John made a face. "I'm a mechanic, not an interior decorator," he said to Hope.

"What do you expect?" I asked, nodding towards John. "Look at the way he's dressed."

Hope laughed. "Oh, come on," she

protested. "He's not really going to the wedding like *that*..." She turned to John. "Are you?"

John pretended to be hurt. "What's wrong with the way I'm dressed?" he demanded. He held up his hands. Usually they were black with grease but that day you could actually see that he had lines on his palms. "I'm clean, aren't I?"

I sat across from Hope. "Don't tell me," I said to John. "You don't like weddings either."

"That's not true," said John. He put three mugs of coffee on the table. "I think weddings are great." He grinned. "As long as they're not mine."

"Or mine," said my mother, suddenly appearing in the doorway. She was still in the old football jersey she wore as a nightgown. "Wouldn't you know it?" she asked, pointing out of the window. It was still raining. "Happy is the bride the sun shines on."

Hope looked at me.

"My mother doesn't believe in weddings," I explained. "She'd rather go to a funeral."

Hope looked at my mother. "Really?"

My mother went over and took a mug from the rack on the wall. "Really." She poured herself some coffee.

"She's right," agreed John. "The food's better and you can be pretty sure things won't

84

get worse."

He and my mother thought this was hilarious.

Hope tried to ignore them. "Jeez," she breathed. "I love weddings." She poured milk into her mug. "So does my mom. When I was little we'd always stop when we passed a wedding to watch the bride and groom come out of the church, whether we knew them or not."

My mother and John exchanged a look. "It's probably better if you don't know them," said my mother. "That way you won't be upset when they get divorced."

They both thought this was pretty funny, too.

I turned to Hope. "They're as bad as each other," I moaned. "John's a terminal bachelor, and my mother's a born-again old maid."

"It's too bad it's not Halloween," said Hope, as she turned the car around and we started back down Smoke Hole Road.

"Halloween?" I repeated. I didn't see what Halloween had to do with anything. A sunny day would have been nice. Then at least we wouldn't be driving blind through the downpour. The Beetle's windshield wipers weren't overly efficient.

"Sure," said Hope. "Then we could just knock on every door till we found the right house." She ploughed slowly through a deep puddle. "Or if we were in the Girl Scouts," she added. "Selling cookies."

"It's too bad we don't live in a city," I countered. City blocks were manageable and controlled. They didn't stretch on for miles and miles the way the roads in the mountains did. So far we'd been up and down Smoke Hole Road and Jefferson Way about twenty times and still we hadn't found the mailbox with Copeland on the side. We were both soaking wet from taking turns to get out and look.

Hope braked suddenly in front of a mailbox that looked like a cow. "I think we should ask," she said.

I glanced over. "Ask?"

Hope nodded. "Sure." She pointed up a muddy trail that led to a large wooden house with a sun deck. "We go up to the door and say we're looking for the Copelands." She gave me one of her most hopeful smiles. "What could be easier?" she wanted to know. "People do it all the time."

Not on Smoke Hole Road, they didn't.

We tried four houses in a row. At the first two, the women had never heard of the Copelands. At the third, the man wouldn't even open the door. At the fourth, the man announced that he wasn't buying anything, before we could open our mouths, and then he slammed the door in our faces.

I wasn't so sure about the fifth house Hope

86

wanted to try. It had two sun decks on different levels, a driveway about a mile long with a *Beware of the Bull Terrier* sign at one end, and about half a dozen late-model cars parked in front of the three-door garage at the other. We left the Beetle on the road.

"Maybe we should skip this one," I suggested as we trudged to the house through the deluge. "These people look really rich. They're not going to know anyone normal unless it's the mailman."

Hope gave my arm a tug. "Maybe their servants have heard of them, then," said Hope.

I'd half expected a butler to answer our ring, but instead it was answered by a little boy and a brown-and-white dog that was throwing itself against the storm door in a pretty alarming way. It looked to me like it was foaming at the mouth.

The dog barked hysterically. The boy didn't say anything.

"We're looking for the Copelands," Hope shouted sweetly.

The dog went nuts – or more nuts. The little boy just stared.

"The Copelands!" bellowed Hope. "Do you know the Copelands?"

The dog grabbed hold of the doorknob with its teeth and hung there, swinging and clawing wildly. The little boy turned and ran.

"This is ridiculous," I whispered. "Let's go

before his mother comes out." Or the dog managed to open the door.

"Too late," said Hope.

A crisp blonde woman wearing a lot of gold jewellery had stepped through the doorway at the end of the hall and was coming toward us with a polite smile on her face. When she reached the door she took hold of the dog's collar and pulled him away without even a wobble in her smile.

"Stop it, Gringo," she ordered. "Behave yourself." Gringo collapsed at her feet. She turned back to us. "I understand you're looking for me."

Looking for her? I opened my mouth and shut it again. Was she saying that she was *Mrs Copeland*? Was she saying that we'd found Bill's house?

Fortunately, Hope still had the power of speech. "You're Mrs Copeland?" she asked in her most grown-up voice.

"Yes, I—" Mrs Copeland hesitated, as if she were trying to figure out how Hope knew who she was. And then she touched a hand to her forehead. "Oh, of course!" A real smile lit up her face. "You're from the charity shop!" She opened the storm door and started waving us in. "It's very good of you to come on a Saturday," she was saying. "Especially in this weather." She peered out at the driveway. "There's quite a lot," she was saying. "Is it only the two of you? Do you have a van?"

Hope and I looked at each other. Now what were we going to do?

Mrs Copeland went on, oblivious to the stunned silence around her. "I must say, it's good to see girls your age interested in more than boys and clothes for a change." She gave us another smile.

I groaned silently. I hadn't even met Bill yet and already I was deceiving his mother. I didn't really think this was the right way to start a major relationship.

Hope kicked me.

I forced myself to speak. "I—We—"

But Mrs Copeland didn't notice that I was trying to speak. She kept right on going. "I think it's very commendable that you give up some of your free time to help others."

Hope gave me another kick.

I forced myself to speak again. "I—We—"

But still Mrs. Copeland didn't stop talking. "I don't know," she was saying, shaking her head, "but a lot of the young girls I meet seem a little …" she shrugged, "well, shallow, I guess." She laughed. "Or maybe it's just the girls my son brings home."

The girls my son brings home… There was no way I could say anything now. I thought my heart was going to implode.

Hope rallied. If you could call it rallying.

"We do this every Saturday," she said

brightly. "It's our good deed for the week."

"It's our good deed for the week," I mimicked as we shut the doors on the Beetle and Hope started the engine.

Hope gave herself a shake. If we'd been wet before, we qualified as drowned-at-sea by the time we'd finished hauling the Copelands' old clothes and bric-a-brac to the car in the rain, a job made even harder because every time I picked up a box or a bag, Gringo attached himself to the other end. He obviously didn't like me any more than I liked him.

"I mean, really, Hope. Couldn't you have thought of something better than that?" I readjusted the box on my lap and nodded towards the mound of bags and boxes squeezed into the back of the car. "Something that would have let her know we weren't from the charity shop?"

"Well, I didn't hear you saying anything more intelligent," grumbled Hope. "You were just standing there grunting." She rubbed steam from the windshield with her hand.

"Yeah, but what happens when the real collectors from the charity shop turn up?" I demanded. "Huh, Miss Genius? What happens then?"

"Who cares?" asked my best friend, switching on the wipers.

"I care," I said a little loudly. "What happens

when I do meet Bill and we start going out? I can never go over to the house to meet his mother, can I? She'll have me arrested as a thief. Or for fraud. I'm sure that impersonating a charity worker is a federal offence."

"Oh, please…" moaned Hope. "By the time that happens she'll've forgotten she ever saw you before."

We had to go back. Not next week. Not next month. Not next year. We had to go back that afternoon. Mr Copeland had left an address book in a suit jacket. The woman in the charity shop had been so thrilled when we told her we were delivering the stuff from the Copelands that she'd started ripping open boxes right then and there. She found the book when it fell on the floor. "Oh, dear," she said. "It's lucky we found that, isn't it?" She handed the address book to me. "You'll see that gets back to Mrs Copeland, won't you?"

"Why don't you take it up to the house?" I suggested to Hope. "It doesn't take two people to carry a tiny little book like that a few metres. I'll wait in the car."

"Oh no, you won't." Hope pushed the car door open. "I'm doing this for you. You're coming with me."

"But, Hope," I protested as she climbed out into the rain. "If I go back so soon she's bound to remember me."

Hope looked in at me through the driver's side. "Out!" she ordered.

I got out.

The worst thing that could have happened wasn't that Mrs Copeland would never forget me, having seen me twice in one afternoon. The worst thing was that Mrs Copeland wasn't home.

Bill answered the door. He was wearing dark purple tracksuit bottoms, a baggy long-sleeved black T-shirt, and a black suede vest; and his hair was hanging loose. He was talking on a mobile phone. He looked like a young god. The young god of gym and advanced-technology communication.

My automatic nervous system shut down. I stopped breathing. I stopped thinking. I didn't move. The only thing I kept doing was looking. At Him. His mouth was fuller than I'd remembered. His eyes were bluer. His special-ness was more intense.

"Yeah, that sounds great," he was saying into the phone as he opened the storm door. "I've got some stuff to do in the afternoon, and I have to eat, so eight's OK." He turned to us and raised one eyebrow. "Yeah?" he mouthed. His eyes met mine.

It never happened like this in movies or songs. If we'd been in a movie or a song – or even a TV commercial – when he said "Yeah?" I would have said "Hi." And that would have been that. Sparks. Earth tremors. Pheromones all over the place, like just-born turtles heading for the sea.

But I wasn't in a movie. Not unless it was *Nightmare on Smoke Hole Road*.

Gringo must have been in the backyard, because all of a sudden he came around the side of the house. The second he saw us he started running, barking like crazy.

I didn't say anything. I just shoved the address book at Bill, grabbed Hope's hand, and ran.

I'd promised myself that I'd spend some of Sunday working on my English paper. Or at least coming up with an idea for my English paper. Bone was comparing *Peter Pan* to *The Lost Boys,* but I hadn't thought of anything yet. I'd been too busy thinking about how I was going to meet Bill.

And then that Sunday I was too busy thinking about how I was never going to meet Bill – and how if I did meet him, it would be a disaster.

I'd napalmed my chances. If Bill saw me again he wouldn't think, *Wow! That's the girl of my dreams!* He'd think, *Hey, isn't that the crazy girl who came to the house and ran away?* Or, worse still, he'd think, *Hey, isn't that the girl who stole our old clothes?*

My mother didn't notice that my life was

over. She must have gotten home really late because she didn't get out of bed until one. She stood in my doorway for a while, talking about the wedding, but I was only half listening. Weddings just made me think of Bill. Then she went over to John's for brunch, mumbling about fixing his toilet or something. When she got back, she collapsed on the couch and spent the rest of the day reading the paper and watching TV.

At about seven o'clock I came out of my room. I thought a little television might stop me from feeling so miserable. You know, divert my attention.

My mother looked up from the Sunday magazine she'd been leafing through. "How do models do it?" she wanted to know. "I smiled so much yesterday my jaw hurts."

My jaw hurt, too, but from grinding my teeth. It was something I did whenever I was really upset.

"I must say, though," my mother went on, "Marilyn was as happy as any woman I've ever seen." She looked down at the colour supplement on her lap. "Let's hope it works for her this time."

"Um," I mumbled as my own future continued to dissolve in front of my eyes. My life was over. I would never be happy again. I stared at the screen. A couple who had been shouting at each other the second before were suddenly swept into a passionate embrace. I ground my teeth. It wasn't working. I was going to cry.

The doorbell rang.

My mother glanced over the back of the sofa. "That's the delivery boy," she said. "I couldn't face cooking tonight. You want to pay him, Mike?"

I didn't want to pay him. I didn't want to eat. I didn't want anything but to crawl into some hole and stay there for the rest of my life. There was nothing left to live for. I'd lost my chance of real true love.

The doorbell rang again. "Mike," said my mother. "Will you please answer the door?"

I took my mother's wallet from the coffee table and forced myself off the sofa. I crossed the room. I opened the door.

I guess that, until that moment, I hadn't really understood how Fate works. Hope and I had been trying to help Fate along, but Fate hadn't wanted our help. Fate works alone.

Bill Copeland was standing there, just a few inches away from me, smiling under the porch light.

It took every bit of self-control I had not to slam the door in his face.

He held up a black-and-silver bag and smiled. "Chez Moi." And then he smiled again, but this time his smile was almost shy. "Do I know you?" he asked. He stepped back and looked at the house, as though this would answer his question. He shook his head. "I'm sorry," he said, "but you look really familiar. Have I delivered here before?"

My heart started beating again. He didn't recognize me. Not specifically. Not in an *Aren't you the girl who told my mother she was collecting for the charity shop?* way.

"No," I mumbled. "No, you've never delivered here before."

"Really?" He frowned, trying to remember why I looked so familiar.

I held my breath. Any second now he was going to have this image of me in a bright yellow parka with my hair dripping wet. And then Fate changed her mind about how she'd been treating me over the last week. Instead of making him remember that the last time he'd seen me I'd been pelting down his driveway, dragging Hope behind me, she inspired me. "Wait a minute." I almost laughed. "I think you're right. I think I do know you. Aren't you a friend of Mark Bone's?"

"Yeah, I am." His frown turned to a happy grin. It was the loveliest thing I'd ever seen. "That's right ... I knew I recognized you! You used to hang out with Mark's little brother."

The word "little" made me want to drop through the floor, but I managed not to panic. "Bobby," I more or less whispered.

"Bobby." He handed me the bag. "That'll

be $21.98." He winked. "I'd never forget a face like yours." He winked again. "Even though you've grown up…"

He said it so quickly and quietly that I wasn't sure that I'd heard him right. Had he really said I'd grown up? Had he really said, "I'd never forget a face like yours"? Or had he said something else? Something like, "That's what it costs for door to door"? I couldn't very well ask him to repeat it, though, so I just stood there staring at him, the money in my hand, trying to will him to say it again.

"Michelle!" boomed my mother. Someone with bad hearing could have heard her. "Michelle! What on earth is taking you so long? Pay the boy. I'd like to eat tonight."

I handed him a twenty and a ten.

"Thanks." He gave me another smile. My idea of lovely stepped up a few notches. "Michelle."

A shiver ran through me. It was as though I'd never heard my name before. *Michelle*. Why hadn't I ever liked that name? When Bill said it, it sounded almost musical.

I smiled back. "Just keep the change."

WHEN LOVE
COMES TO TOWN

My mother was furious about the tip I'd given "the delivery boy". She moaned about it all night long. "Eight bucks!" she kept saying. "Eight bucks! It's not like he had to walk out here in a blizzard, you know." She said there was already a delivery charge worked in with the price; I didn't have to give a nearly fifty percent tip on top. She said I'd be a little less generous when it was my hard-earned money I was spending and not hers.

Hope said she would have done the same thing I had.

"What else could you do?" she asked again at lunch on Monday. I was too excited not to say anything in front of Bone. Things were getting serious now. If he didn't like it, it was just too bad.

Bone was reading while he ate, not even glancing at us, but this didn't affect his hearing any. "I bet you wouldn't have given me eight bucks if I'd been the delivery boy," said Bone.

"There was nothing else I could do," I said, answering Hope. "I was terrified my mom was going to come to the door and embarrass me even more. And, anyway, I got so confused when he said he wouldn't forget my face—"

"But he did forget it," broke in Bone. "He didn't remember seeing you in the restaurant when you went with your mom ... he didn't remember seeing you the time I brought you there ... he didn't remember seeing you at his own front door..."

"What are you suggesting?" I snapped. "That he was just handing me a line?"

Bone's eyes didn't move from the page in front of them. "No, Mike. I'm suggesting he has amnesia."

I pretended I hadn't heard him. I went back to Hope. "And when he said my name..." My voice turned into a sigh. I could still hear it in my mind. *Michelle*... It made my skin tingle.

Bone finally looked up. "Mike?" he half laughed. "Bill Copeland calling you Mike made your brain turn to Velveeta?"

I made a face at him. "He didn't call me Mike," I informed him coolly. "He called me Michelle."

Bone made a face back. "I thought you hated Michelle," he sneered. "I thought you said it reminded you of that cheesy Beatles song."

"It depends who's saying it," I answered pointedly. I wanted to make sure Bone knew I didn't mean him. I turned back to Hope. "The problem is, when am I going to see him next? My mother's never going to order anything from Chez Moi again. She made that pretty clear."

"Maybe she will—"

I cut her off. "No she won't." What my mother had said was that she couldn't believe that first I ordered the wrong food and then I overpaid. What, was I on the Chez Moi payroll or something?

"So we'll go Friday after we pick up the videos," Hope decided. "They have cakes and stuff like that. We'll get our snacks there." She grinned. "I bet he's hoping you come in," she said.

Bone picked up his book again. "The only thing Bill Copeland's ever hoped for in his life is a basketball season pass," said Bone.

Monday night was as long as a year. My mother spent most of it on the telephone while Leonardo and I sat in the living-room, trying to come up with a topic for my English paper. I could hear her in the kitchen, laughing and yapping away. She'd certainly cheered up now that Marilyn's wedding was over. I drew a broken heart on a clean sheet of paper. Then I balled it up and threw it on the floor with the others. The only wedding that would ever cheer me up was mine.

"So how's it going?" asked my mother when she finally resurfaced from her phone call.

Paranoia had weakened my defences. *What if Bone was right?* I wondered. *What if Bill was just handing me a line?* "What do you think?" I asked. "Do you think if someone tells you he'd never forget a face like yours that he's sincere, or is he just handing you a line?"

She looked at me for a few seconds, as if she were trying to figure out what was causing a boiler to overheat. "I know what you could do for your paper," she said at last. "You could compare *When Harry Met Sally* with *Romeo and Juliet.*"

"*When Harry Met Sally?*" I really couldn't believe her sometimes. "But that's so unrealistic! Best friends don't fall in love like that."

"They don't?" asked my mother. She wasn't laughing, but she was smiling. "Why not?"

"Because they don't," I spluttered. "It'd be like me falling in love with Bone!"

"I don't see what's so funny about that," said my mother. "There's nothing wrong with Bobby."

"But he's my friend! I know him too well to fall in love with him. Love's like a thunderbolt not an old coat."

"Old coats last a lot longer than bolts of thunder," said my mother.

101

By Tuesday morning I was a wreck. It had taken me hours to get to sleep on Monday night, thinking about Bill, and when I finally did I'd dreamed about him. Only, even though I knew it was Bill, he looked like Bone. "Why do you look like Bone?" I kept asking him. "Why don't you look like you?" It freaked me so much that I woke up. But I could still see Bone's face, smiling into mine. I figured that if I didn't get another glimpse of Bill soon I really would forget what he looked like.

Hope said I needed to cheer up. She suggested that we go shopping. Hope believes in shopping as a cure for depression. She said that even if it didn't make me feel any better right now, I'd need something new for when Bill did ask me out.

I said, "Sometimes I wish your parents had called you something normal like Linda or Judith." But I thought it was a good idea anyway. Anything was better than doing nothing.

Bone looked at us over his sandwich. "You want me to do *what*?"

"Take us to the mall," said Hope. "It's therapy for Mike."

Bone made a distressed kind of face. "But why me? I hate the mall." This was true. Among all the things Bone hated, the mall was right at the top of the list. The only time Bone went near the mall was when his mother dragged him with her to buy clothes he didn't want, or when he went to the exotic-pet store to get Leonardo his birthday and his Christmas presents.

"Because my mom's using the Bug today," Hope told him for the second time.

Of course, Bone turned on me. "I thought you were coming over to listen to my new B.B. King album this afternoon," he said accusingly. "You promised."

I decided to grovel. "Please, Bone," I begged. "As a special favour? I'll come over tomorrow … or the next day…"

Bone looked thoughtful. "Tomorrow's no good, and I've got an all-day session with the band on Saturday, so I want to work on my English paper the rest of the week…"

"OK," I said, trying to stay patient and calm. "Just tell me when."

Bone gave me a look. It was the look of a person who is about to say that he'll do something you want him to do, but who wants you to know that that doesn't mean he's happy about it.

"Sunday," said Bone. "You'll come over Sunday, right?" He turned to Hope. "Why don't you come, too? I've got some Cajun fiddle music I want you to hear."

"That sounds great," said Hope. "I'd love to." She laughed. "To tell you the truth, I'm getting a little tired of playing classical music. Maybe you're right after all. Maybe I should branch out a little."

"Of course I'm right," Bone assured her. "I have this hunch about you…"

I stared at them in wonderment. Here I was, tormented by love, and they were talking about music. In a minute they'd be humming bars of their favourite songs to each other.

"So you'll do it?" I cut in. "You'll take us to the mall after school?"

Bone squinched up his mouth again. "Yeah, I'll do it." He sighed. "But you're paying for the gas."

Bone abandoned us as soon as we got to the mall.

"I'm going down to the ocean," he announced from the truck. "There's no way I'm trudging around with you two while you look at clothes. I'd rather go to a ten-hour Janet Jackson concert." He pointed to the left. "I'll meet you over there, in the pizza place, in an hour."

An hour is a long time if you're at the dentist's, but it isn't very long when you're shopping for the perfect outfit for your first date with the boy of your dreams. One day might have been enough, but one hour was cutting it close. With fifteen minutes before rendezvous time, Hope and I were still only in the mall's west wing. Hope had gotten herself a couple of CDs and a white blouse she needed for the county orchestra, but I was still trying on clothes.

"What do you think?" I asked Hope's reflection in the full-length mirror. She was standing beside me, looking thoughtful.

"I'm not sure." She tilted her head. "I like the skirt." The skirt was a straight black one in the same material as tracksuit pants. Dressed up, but casual. "But I'm not sure about the top." The top was a floral grandad shirt with a frilly neckline. "The ruffle makes you look a little young." She tilted her head to one side. "Try this one."

She handed me a long-sleeved baggy T-shirt that was hand dyed an incredibly intense shade of yellow.

I twisted to the left. I twisted to the right. I turned my back to the mirror and looked over my shoulder. It looked all right. In fact, it looked better than all right. It looked like it had been made for me. Except that I was in my socks, I looked like a girl in an ad for Dr Martens. Coolly casual and sophisticated.

"I like it," Hope decided. "I really like it. It's under-stated, but stylish. Plus, it brings out your colouring." She snapped her fingers. "I know. You can borrow my suede vest when you do go out with him. It'll look great with that shirt."

"Done!" I said. I started changing back into my clothes. "Let's pay for this and get out of here before Bone leaves us behind."

There was a line about a mile long for the cashier.

Hope glanced at her watch. "I better go meet Bobby," said Hope. "I'll tell him you're on your way."

The line moved slowly, but I didn't really mind. I was imagining my first date with Bill: The doorbell rang. I went to answer it. I opened the door. Bill was standing there. He was casually but stylishly dressed, too. Only he didn't look like he was in an ad for Doc Martens. He looked like a rock star. He'd been getting ready to smile, but when he saw me his expression changed to something like awe, which matched the expression of awe on my face. "Jeez," he whispered. "You look so ... so ... you look terrific." Our eyes locked. "So do you," I whispered back.

I don't really remember paying for the skirt and shirt. I just sort of drifted out into the plaza, holding the bag against my chest. Now in my mind, Bill was driving me home. His arm brushed mine as he changed gears. Tina Turner started singing on the radio "You're Simply The Best". He glanced over at me. I glanced over at him. We smiled at the same time. "I think they're playing our song," he said.

One minute I was floating toward the pizzeria, imagining Bill's first kiss, and the next I'd collided with a flannel shirt. My face was so close to it that I could have bitten off one of the buttons.

"Woof!" I gasped.

"Are you all right?" asked this melted-chocolate voice.

I looked up. Looking down at me with a worried expression on his face was a vision in perfectly faded jeans and a blue flannel shirt. The silver lizard in his ear glinted in the light shining through the glass roof of the mall like a star. *It can't be Him*, I told myself. *I'm dreaming. I must have hit him so hard I got concussion.*

The worried expression changed to a smile. "It is you," said Bill, disengaging me from his chest. "I thought it was but I wasn't sure. You didn't look up when I called you." He laughed. "I was a little surprised that you just walked into me like that."

I couldn't speak. I was still feeling his hands on my shoulders.

"You remember me, don't you?" he asked. "I delivered your supper Sunday night."

"Of course I remember you," I blurted out. And then I started babbling. "I—I'm sorry. I'm really sorry," I apologized. "I don't know where my mind was ... I didn't mean to—"

He put his hands on my shoulders again. "It's OK, Michelle. I like girls who are unpredictable." He blinded me with another smile. "Were you going somewhere, or are you just hanging around?"

My heart had been making the racket it always made when I saw Bill, but now it stopped dead. *Why is he asking me that?* I wondered. *Is he going to ask me to go for a soda or something?* I knew what I should say. I should say that I was on my way to meet Hope and Bone.

I shrugged. "No, I wasn't going anywhere special." I held up my bag. "I just finished my shopping."

"Really? Me too." He held up the bag he was carrying. "I had to buy another shirt for work. I tipped a hot fudge sundae on myself and the housekeeper couldn't get the chocolate stains out."

"Gee," I said. "That's too bad."

Bill shrugged philosophically. "That's all part of the fun of being a waiter." He glanced around almost nervously. Then he looked back at me. "So," he said. He cleared his throat. "How are you getting home?" He cleared his throat again. "I could give you a ride if you want. Maybe we could stop for a soda or something on the way back."

My heart lurched. I was tingling so much I felt as though someone must have plugged me in. He was offering me a lift! He wanted to drive me home! Just him and me. Together. In his car. It's no wonder that I couldn't think straight. I mean, I did know what I should say to that, too. I should thank him and tell him that it was all right, I had a ride. With Hope and Bone. But I couldn't seem to get the words to my mouth. Not while my brain was shrieking, *He wants to drive me home! He wants to drive me home!*

And, anyway, I knew that Hope would understand.

Bill's car was a customized Cherokee, metallic purple with purple-and-red tail-lights and a strip of purple lights under the running boards. Normally, I preferred old cars with character, but that was because I didn't really have any choice. That was all anybody I knew had.

"Wow," I said admiringly, as he opened the door for me. "It's beautiful. There isn't even one drop of rust on it and there's nothing about to fall off."

"Of course not," said Bill. "It's only six months old."

Since he hadn't gotten the rust joke, I decided not to say that I wasn't used to riding in cars that weren't at least as old as I was. I smiled. "Purple's my favourite colour," I said, instead.

"Really? Most of the girls I know like pastels." He grinned. "My favourite colour's purple, too."

I grinned back, encouraged. "I really like your lizard," I rushed on. "I'm very fond of lizards."

He looked pleased. "I thought it was different. You know, instead of a hoop. Everybody wears hoops."

I put my foot on the running board and started to climb into the jeep. I was just about to throw myself into the seat when something large and heavy flung itself against me, as though it were trying to get through my body. I might have thought it was a really big rock if it hadn't been barking. I screamed.

"Gringo!" shouted Bill. "Gringo, get down!"

Gringo stayed where he was, which was on top of me, drooling in my face. Maybe Bill didn't remember seeing me at his house, but his dog did.

"Just push him off," ordered Bill. "He won't hurt you."

I couldn't see how he could be so sure of that. Not the way Gringo was barking and dripping saliva all over me. I gave him a shove. It was like pushing a redwood.

"Harder," said Bill. "He's just playing." He laughed. "You're not afraid of dogs, are you?"

"Of course not," I answered quickly. I didn't add that I was willing to make an exception in this case.

I shoved harder. Gringo put his paws on my shoulders as if he wanted to dance.

Bill leaned over me. He was so close you'd have thought he was going to kiss me. Either that or he was trying to smell what I'd had for lunch. But, of course, he wasn't doing either of those things. He grabbed hold of Gringo's collar and hauled him off. "You just sit in the back and behave," he said sternly. Gringo licked his face.

As soon as he got behind the wheel, Bill started talking about the jeep. I sat smiling at the side of his face, one eye on the back of the car in case his dog decided to jump me again. Bill's parents had given him the Cherokee for his birthday. It had special brakes and special suspension and it was as comfortable as a BMW. I didn't understand what he said about the brakes and the suspension, but I figured that they must be what made riding in Bill's jeep so different from riding in Mrs Perez's Beetle or my mom's van or Bone's pickup, so I just nodded and said, "Um." I didn't know if the jeep was more comfortable than a BMW, either, since I'd never been in a BMW, but it was definitely a lot more comfortable than the Bug or the van or the truck, so I nodded to that, too. I was impressed that Bill seemed to know so much about cars. So much for Bone saying Bill was only interested in basketball.

There was a sudden silence after he told me

about the suspension. I could hear the engine and the wheels and my heart, but it was still so quiet I almost thought I'd gone deaf. I glanced away so Bill wouldn't know I was looking at him. I got the impression he'd finished talking for a while.

Say something, I ordered myself. *Show him how fascinating and intelligent you are.* I cleared my throat. "So," I croaked. "Why don't you wear a watch?"

"Very observant." He grinned at the road ahead of us. "Why don't you?"

"I don't like being a slave to time." I couldn't tell from his expression if he understood what I meant or not. "You know, I hate the way people are always checking their watches instead of enjoying the minute they're in," I explained.

Bill nodded. "That's cool," he said. "That's a really good way of putting it."

I didn't admit that it was actually Bobby Bone who had put it that way. "Really?" I said. "You think so, too?"

He looked over at me. "Great minds think alike," said Bill. He winked. "I knew I was going to like you."

I didn't say, *And I knew I was going to like you, too,* but I thought it.

A bright yellow sports car zoomed past us. "Imagine spending fifty thousand on a great car like that and getting it in yellow," said Bill.

"Yellow's so, I don't know ... childish. You can't really take it seriously."

I said, "Um," and kicked the bag with my new yellow top in it under my seat in case he glanced over and saw its colour.

After a few miles I began to realize that it wasn't only the suspension that made riding in the Cherokee different from riding in the Beetle or the pickup or the van. It was Bill. Being with him was like having the flu. My skin was hot and damp, my chest was tight, I was lightheaded and weak. I was sure my face was flushed.

"So you still friends with Mark's brother, Bobby?" Bill asked as we pulled into the McDonald's parking lot.

"Yeah," I said. "We're still friends."

"You know, I ran into him the other day outside the restaurant," Bill went on. "I haven't seen him for a couple of years, but he was exactly the same. What a kid!" I decided that if his voice was like melted chocolate, his laugh was more like hot butterscotch sauce. "Still weirder than Mars."

In less than half an hour I'd three times been put in a situation where I knew exactly what I should say, but I also knew that I wasn't going to say it. Like then. I should have said that I didn't think Bone was weird – that he was one of my two best friends – only I didn't. What I said was "A lot of the kids at school think

Bone's weird, but he's really OK. He's very smart. And talented. He—"

Bill's laughter drowned me out. "OK? The way he acts and talks and dresses – and that piece of junk he drives? You really don't think he's weird?"

I laughed, too. "Well, maybe Bone's a little eccentric—" I began.

"He's got 'No Fear' painted on the hood of that wreck." Bill hooted. "What's that supposed to mean?"

"It's a joke," I said quickly. *No Fear* was the kind of thing guys airbrushed on their Harleys. Which was why Bone had put it on a twenty-year-old Ford pickup that couldn't go over forty without something falling off.

"And that music of his!" Bill laughed. He jumped out his side.

I opened my door. I was just about to jump down but I stopped.

"Is he still into that awful music?" Bill had suddenly appeared beside me.

Good grief, I thought. *He's going to help me out.* It was too romantic for words.

I took his outstretched hand. "Oh, yeah," I said. "He's a really good guitarist now. He—"

"He used to drive Mark nuts with it." Bill slammed my door closed. "He played it constantly. It was so depressing."

This time I really was going to say what I should say, what Bone would have said and what I believed – that the blues aren't depressing, they're honest and real, not manufactured like pop songs – but I didn't have the chance. Bill lightly touched my elbow to steer me towards the entrance, and my brain disconnected itself from my throat.

He's touching me, I thought as we walked through the glass doors. *He's really touching me!*

"Not that I don't like some blues," Bill was saying. "I like the Stones, they're cool – but Bobby's stuff was all one guy moaning and a five-string guitar."

I laughed at the joke. Everybody knew that guitars had six strings or twelve. "He likes the Stones, too, now," I said as we reached the counter.

Bill looked over at me. "What'll you have?"

I stared into his smile. "Huh?"

"You want a burger or some chicken nuggets?"

"Ah," I said. "Oh, no, I – I don't eat meat."

"See, I knew right away you were different." His smile almost glowed. "You're a vegetarian? That's really cool. I stopped eating red meat for a while myself, but it made me feel really weak."

And being with you makes me feel really weak, I said to myself. Out loud, I said, "Oh."

"So what do you usually get?" asked Bill. "The fish thing?"

I was staring up at the menu. Blankly. Mc*this* … Mc*that* … it was hard to tell what was actually being sold. I almost wished the menu were in French, "I don't usually get anything," I answered in desperation. "I've never been in a McDonald's before."

Bill laughed so loudly that everyone else at the counter looked at us. "You what?" he choked. His voice was practically echoing. *"You've never been in McDonald's?"*

At this rate I was afraid it wouldn't take long for me to go from being "different" to being "weird," like Mark's little brother.

"My mother says McD stands for Mindless Corporate Destruction," I explained. "She won't let them have any of her money because of what they've done to destroy the rainforests." Among other things.

Bill had stopped laughing and was gazing at me in what can only be described as wonderment. "You mean you really never have been in McDonald's before?" He whistled. "You know, lots of girls *look* like they might be different, but you really are different, aren't you?" He grinned happily. "This is like being with someone from another planet."

I guess he must have been inspired by his Big Mac and fries because Bill talked about work all the way home.

"Staff's the biggest problem," he informed

me. "If you have good staff, you're halfway there."

I thought of the waitress with the perfect looks. Had he ever asked her out? "Well, you certainly have some very pretty staff at Chez Moi," I joked.

"You mean Lara?" He gave me a glance. "She's not as pretty as you," he said quickly, his eyes darting back to the road. He laughed. "And she's not a great waitress, either. She's always taking off."

She's not as pretty as you... That had to mean he'd never been interested in her. Relief made me generous. "She seemed OK to me," I said.

"That's because you don't have to work with her," said Bill. "I'm telling you, this job has already taught me a lot. You really have to know what you're doing to make a success of a restaurant like Chez Moi. You wouldn't believe how complicated it is."

"It can't be easy to bring a taste of Paris to the redwoods," I said, laughing.

Bill grinned. "You like our slogan?" he asked. "That's a Copeland original."

"You mean *you*?" Thank God he hadn't realized I was being sarcastic. "That's your line?"

He nodded. "That's right. And a lot of the decor was mine, too." He grinned sheepishly. "Well, mine and my mother's."

I was lost. I couldn't quite picture Bill's mother in her gold jewellery and expensive clothes waiting on tables. "You mean your mother works there, too?"

That cracked him up. "No, she's an interior decorator," he explained when he'd stopped laughing enough to speak. "My father had her design Chez Moi."

I'd thought Bill was just a waiter, but he wasn't. He was learning the business from the bottom up. "After a year or so, my father's going to make me manager," he told me. "Once I've learned the ropes."

"You mean your father owns Chez Moi?"

Bill nodded. "Among other things. But it's mine when I finish college." We turned up my road. "I'd like to make it a chain." He glanced over at me. "What about your parents? What do they do?"

Thank God one of my parents had a normal job. "My father's a teacher," I said. "But he doesn't live with us. He lives in Seattle." I pointed across the steering wheel. "That's it on the left. The blue one."

We pulled up in front of my house. The van was parked in the driveway.

"Looks like you've got a backed-up sink," said Bill.

"No," I said, "that's my mother's van."

Bill laughed. "No, really. Because if you're having trouble, my dad knows a great

118

plumber."

"My mother is a great plumber," I said loyally. "She's the best there is."

He turned to me with this really surprised look. "You're serious? Your mother's not just a radical vegetarian, she's a plumber as well?" The look of surprise turned to something more like delight. "You really are amazing, aren't you?"

Hope understood why I'd gone home with Bill. She said she would probably have done the same thing herself if she'd been in my shoes. She said it wouldn't have mattered except that she and Bone got a little worried. After all, the papers were always full of stories about girls disappearing from malls. She said it was Bobby who was really upset. He'd dragged her into every store we'd been in, just to make sure I hadn't gone back for something. And then he wanted to call the police. She stopped him only by saying they should wait till they got home to see if I'd turned up or not.

"Bill thinks Bone's weird," I said. "Maybe he's right."

Hope was silent for a few seconds, and then she said, "You don't think maybe he has a – you know, a crush on you, do you?"

Even though the only other person in the closet with me was Leonardo, I could feel myself blush. "Well … I do think he likes me… he kept saying how different I am … and he did say I was pretty … but I wouldn't say he exact—"

Hope sighed. "No, not Bill, Mike. Bone."

"Bone?" It took a few seconds for me to understand what she was saying. "You think *Bone* has a crush on me?" I laughed so hard that Leonardo went into his shell.

"Well, I know it sounds a little crazy," said Hope. "But he was so worked up when you didn't show. You should've seen him, Mike. He said he'd never be able to eat cornflakes again because your picture would be on all the milk cartons: *When Was the Last Time You Saw This Girl?* He really thought something had happened to you."

"Oh, please," I gasped. "Bone's very self-dramatizing, that's all. He loves to create scenes."

"Um," said Hope. "Maybe…"

I called Bone after I hung up with Hope.

Bone didn't understand.

"But you knew we were waiting for you," he kept saying. "Why did you go off with Bill when you knew we were waiting?"

"I don't know," I said. "I really don't know. I guess he just caught me by surprise." There was silence on the other end of the line. "I didn't think you'd mind that much," I added. "I figured you'd understand."

"I wouldn't have minded," snapped Bone, "if you'd told us. If you'd told us you were going home with Bill, that would have been fine. Far be it for me to stand between you and your hormones. But you didn't tell us you were going, Mike. You just left me and Hope sitting there like a couple of mall rats with nothing better to do."

Now the silence was on my end of the phone. I'd said I was sorry. I'd told him the truth. I didn't know why I went off with Bill like that. I just couldn't help myself.

"What'd you think, Mike?" Bone went on. "We're not psychic, you know. How did you expect us to figure out that you'd run into Bill Copeland, he'd offered you a ride, and you'd gone home with him?"

"I'm really sorry," I said for about the twenty-eighth time. What more could I say? I hadn't been thinking of what Hope and Bone would think at all. It hadn't even occurred to me to wonder. "I guess I just wasn't thinking."

"Not with your brain, you weren't," snapped Bone. "You didn't have to upset Hope like that, you know. She was really worried."

This was news to me. "Hope was worried?"

"Yeah," he sneered. "Hope was worried. She thought you'd been kidnapped or raped or something."

I frowned at Leonardo. Hope had never lied

121

to me; but Bone had never lied to me, either. "Hope said you were the one who was so worried."

"Yeah, well, that's Hope, isn't it?" asked Bone. "She's too nice; that's Hope's problem. She doesn't like to upset anyone, does she?" He made a sound somewhere between a snort and a sigh. "Unlike you and me."

THIS MAGIC MOMENT

"But what if Bill doesn't ask me out?" I asked Hope glumly over lunch on Wednesday. I'd been so sure he was going to when he took me home that I was already in the house before I realized that he hadn't.

"But he did take your phone number," reasoned Hope. "Why would he take your number if he wasn't going to ask you out?"

Bone suddenly got to his feet. "I hate to miss even half a chapter in the Michelle and Bill story," he said, quickly picking up his things, "especially when it's getting so exciting, but I've got to go to the library. I'll catch you guys later."

"See you," said Hope.

"Bye," I said. I turned back to Hope. "But what if I've died of a broken heart by the time he gets around to it?"

"Stop it," ordered Hope. "Bill's going to ask

you out. He has to. Why wouldn't he?"

I'd given that question a lot of thought since the previous afternoon. In fact, you could probably say that it was the only thing I had given any thought to. I'd played my seventy-two minutes with Bill over in my mind about a million times and it seemed to me that I couldn't have made as good an impression as I'd thought. It was true that I had made him laugh, but not always when I meant to. Except for screaming hysterically when Gringo landed on top of me, I'd been pretty quiet. I hadn't said one really clever or intelligent thing the entire time. If anything, I'd forced him to do all the talking.

"Why wouldn't he ask me out?" I listed a couple of reasons. "Because I don't like his dog. Because I'd never been in McDonald's before." I groaned. "Why didn't I lie about that? Bill must think I'm a total android. I mean, people in Russia have been to McDonald's. People in China. People in the Amazon—"

"I don't think they have McDonald's in the Amazon," said Hope. "Just the cows."

"What am I going to do?" I wailed. "Fate thrust him in my path and what'd I do? I blew it, that's what I did, I totally blew it."

"I thought you said he said he knew he'd like you," said Hope.

I stared at my uneaten sandwich. "That was early on. Before he said I was like someone from a different planet."

Bill called that night. My mother was sighing over her accounts at the kitchen table while I was getting Leonardo's supper ready at the counter.

My mother answered the phone.

"Hello?" she said. And then she said, "Who?" Something in the way she said "Who?" made me look up. My mother nodded in the general direction of the fridge. "Oh, Michelle. She's here. Just a second, I'll get her." She held the receiver out to me. "It's for you."

"Who is it?" I whispered.

"Search me." She winked.

I held the receiver next to my ear. "Hello?" I said.

"Hello," said that melted-chocolate voice. "Michelle?"

Even though I'd been waiting for this call from the moment I saw Bill, I went cold and hot at the same time. I didn't say anything. I meant to say something, but I didn't. I just smiled at the receiver. I could feel my mother watching me. I turned towards the wall.

"Michelle? Are you there? It's me. Bill."

I said, "Umpgh."

"I gave you a ride home from the mall yesterday," he rushed on. "Remember?"

I felt my face turn red. I moved closer to the

wall. My nose was practically touching the door frame. "Of course I remember," I choked out. How could he think I'd forget?

I could hear him breathing. "Well, I was wondering ... well, I thought maybe you'd like to go to the game Friday night."

"The game?"

"Basketball," he said quickly. "I have tickets for the game at SCU Friday night. I thought you might want to come. You like basketball, don't you?"

If anybody else had asked me if I liked basketball, the answer would have been a simple no. I'd never been to a basketball game in my life, and I'd never wanted to go to one. But it was Bill asking, so the answer wasn't that simple. I mean, how did I know I didn't like basketball if I'd never given it a chance? "Um ... uh ... ," I said, trying to speak loud enough so I could hear myself over the racket my heart was making and low enough so my mother couldn't overhear me. "Well, yeah ... I mean, sure ... I mean, that'd be great."

"I'll pick you up at seven." I could feel his smile through the plastic of the telephone. It was warmer than Leonardo's vivarium. "Don't worry," he said. "I remember where you live."

I didn't move after he hung up. I just stood there holding the receiver and staring at the wall. I could still hear him saying, "Well, bye, Michelle. I'll see you Friday." It sounded the way velvet feels when you rub it on your cheek. I was going to pinch myself to make sure I wasn't dreaming. But I didn't have to.

"So who was that?" asked my mother.

Her voice startled me so much that I dropped the phone. I'd actually forgotten she was there for a second.

"Mike?" said my mother. "Who was that? That wasn't Bobby."

"No," I said, retrieving the dangling receiver. "That wasn't Bone." I hung up, trying to think of what I was going to say next.

My heart was stampeding. My stomach was filled with hundreds of butterflies, all flapping around like crazy. I wanted to shout, "Bill! It was Bill! That's who it was! It was Him!" I wanted to dance around the kitchen. I wanted to run to the front door and scream, "He called me! He called me! He asked me to go out!" But I didn't.

"Well?" asked my mother. "Who was it?"

I looked around. She was back at the table, but her eyes were on me, not on her books.

"It was just this boy I know."

My mother smiled. Slyly. "Just this boy you know?"

"Yeah." I nodded. "Just this boy I know."

"Does he have a name?" asked my mother.

I nodded again. "Yeah, he has a name."

127

My mother raised one eyebrow. "Are you going to tell me what it is, or do I have to guess?"

Up until then I figured I'd been doing a pretty good job of sounding casual and matter-of-fact, but I lost it when I tried to say his name. My face went red again. "Bill," I said a little loudly. "His name's Bill."

My mother pretended not to notice. "Bill." She turned back to her accounts. "That's a nice name."

It was amazing how my mother could say something like, "That's a nice name", and make it sound like a question, like what she'd really said was, "And?".

I opened the fridge and put my head in. The cold air and the sight of the cartons of milk and juice on the top shelf made me feel calmer. "He's taking me to a basketball game," I informed the lemonade. "Friday night."

"Friday night," my mom repeated. "What time?"

I grabbed hold of the apple juice. What time? Was there some curfew I hadn't known about? I swung around so fast I nearly dropped the container. "You are going to let me go, aren't you?" I'd still sounded casual and matter-of-fact in my head, but it came out as a squeak. A shrill one. "You're not saying I can't go?"

My mother looked over at me. "All I asked

was what time you were going," she said patiently. "I'm going out myself Friday night. I wanted to be sure I'd be here to meet him."

"Oh," I said. "Oh, right." I started towards the dish drainer for a glass. "Seven. He's picking me up at seven."

"Oh, that's OK. I'm not leaving till eight."

She kept talking as she started tapping numbers into her calculator. My mother was going to a concert with John.

I jumped again when she suddenly said, "So how did you meet this Bill?"

I don't know why I wasn't expecting her to ask me that, but I wasn't. She surprised me so much that I told her the truth. "He works at Chez Moi. He delivered our supper the other night."

She stopped tapping numbers into her calculator. She looked at me again. "Well, at least we know he has enough money to pay for the tickets," said my mother.

"What?" asked Hope. "Mike, I can't understand you. You have to slow down."

I took a deep breath and tried again. "He called!" I pushed a scarf out of my face. "He called, Hope! Can you believe it? He called. Me! Can you believe it, Hope? He called me!" Just the memory of it gave me shivers.

Hope didn't have to ask who.

"Oh, my God!" she shrieked. "Didn't I tell

you he would? When? What'd he say? Did he ask you out? When are you going to see him again?"

"Just now," I answered. "Yes." Then I repeated what he'd said, exactly as he'd said it.

Hope made a sound between a sigh and the whistle on a boiling kettle. "Oh, my God … I told you he was interested, didn't I? I told you you had to trust in Fate."

"I guess God isn't the only one who works in mysterious ways," I said.

"I guess not," said Hope. "So," she went on, "when's he taking you out? Saturday night?"

"No, Friday."

There was a nanosecond of silence, and then Hope said, "Friday?"

I felt bad that I'd said yes to Friday night without even thinking. Not a lot bad, but a little. I should at least have checked with Hope first. I mean, not only did Hope and I have a standing date on Friday nights, but this Friday we were supposed to go to the movies instead of watching videos. There was a new comedy by a Chinese director that we wanted to see. But I figured Hope would understand.

"I'm really sorry," I apologized. "But I just couldn't say no. What if he thought I was just saying I had other plans because I didn't want to go out with him?"

Hope understood. "Don't be silly," she said. "It's no big deal. We have every other Friday night to hang out together. This is different. This is special." She sighed again. "This is the beginning of your destiny."

Bone didn't think it was the beginning of my destiny. He thought it was the beginning of my downfall.

"Basketball?" He wasn't so much smiling as smirking. "You're kidding, right?"

Hope gave him a *Don't start* look, but he didn't catch it. He was too busy grinning at me.

"No," I said evenly. "I'm not kidding. Bill's asked me to the Santa Clara game."

"And you're going?"

I put down my drink. "Of course I'm going."

Bone stopped smiling. He leaned forward, as though he didn't want to miss anything I might say. "If this isn't too personal a question," said Bone, "*why* are you going?"

His question surprised me into honesty. "Because he asked me," I answered. I should have known better.

Bone thought that was just about the funniest thing he'd ever heard in his life. "Because he *asked* you?"

I stared back at him, coldly. "Yes," I said. "I thought it might be interesting."

Bone made one of his sarcastic faces. "And if he'd asked you to go with him to a seal cull,

131

I suppose you would've thought that might be interesting, too?"

Hope threw her napkin at him. "Stop teasing Mike," she ordered. "She's happy. Leave her alone."

"I'm not teasing her," Bone said flatly. He was talking to Hope, but he was still looking at me. "I'm serious. Why would Mike want to go to a basketball game? She doesn't like basketball. She doesn't understand basketball. The only time she's ever seen anyone play was on a TV commercial."

"Maybe she's doing what you're always telling me to do with my music," replied Hope. "Broadening her horizons ... trying something new..."

Bone's eyes stayed on mine. "Going to something you don't like just because you think the person who asks you has a nice smile is not the same as experimenting with a different type of music," he said to Hope. "The latter is intelligent, positive and creative." He leaned back, folding his arms across his chest. "The former is dumb."

"It is not dumb!" I hissed back. I wished I had something to throw at him. Something heavier than a napkin. One of my mother's wrenches, for instance.

"It's the action of a superficial and shallow person," said Bone.

Hope said, "Oh, come on, Bobby. You're

getting carried away."

I stood up. "You just wait till you fall for someone," I said as I shoved in my chair. "We'll see who has the last laugh then."

"*I* will," said Bone. "Falling for someone's never made me change."

"Who do you think he was talking about?" asked Hope.

It was finally Friday. Hope had come home with me to help me find something to wear. I tossed another skirt on to the pile of rejected clothes on the chair. There were more things out of my closet than in it now. The trouble with beginning your destiny is that you want to be wearing the right thing.

"He who?" I asked.

"Bone," said Hope. "When he said falling for someone's never made him change."

I shut the closet and moved on to my bureau. "He didn't mean he'd ever been interested in anyone, if that's what you're getting at. He just meant he wouldn't change if he was."

"No, he didn't," said Hope. Even though my back was to her, I knew she was shaking her head. "He said, 'Falling for someone's never made me change.' I heard him. Those were his exact words."

I flung a few more tops on the chair. "Those may have been his exact words," I said, "but that wasn't what he meant." I took a rose-

133

coloured shirt from the drawer and held it up for inspection. "I knew Bone when his mother still chose his clothes for him," I reminded her. "He's never had a crush on anyone."

"I'm not sure about that," said Hope. "I think he might still have one on you." And then she added, "No, not that one, Mike. It makes you look too young."

"Bone never had a crush on me, and he doesn't have one now," I said firmly. "And if he'd had one on somebody else, he would have told me." I dropped the rose shirt on to the pile. "He's told me about every major first in his life – his first guitar, his first guitar lesson, his first B.B. King album, his first detention, his first wet dream ... all of them."

Hope shrieked. "His first wet dream? Really?"

"Uh-huh." I turned to look at her. "It was a revelation to both of us."

Hope got off the bed. "Well, then it's really strange that he didn't tell you about this girl, isn't it?" she asked.

I threw my arms in the air. "What is it with you?" I demanded. "For the hundredth time, there is no girl."

Hope just stood there staring at me for a couple of seconds. She looked like she was about to say something, but then she changed her mind. She reached into the drawer and pulled out an old body suit. "What about this?" she asked. "Didn't you tell me purple was Bill's favourite color?"

In the end I decided on my purple jeans and a white silk blouse my grandmother had given me in case my mother ever had another child and I needed something to wear to the christening.

As soon as Hope left, I ran myself a bath. I put in some of the scented oil my grandmother gave my mother for Christmas, in case my mother ever met someone and started caring about how she looked. After all, it wasn't likely that my mother was ever going to use it. I dug out a magazine I'd bought on the way home from school. I turned to page 23: "How to Make Him Like You."

According to the article, although I definitely wanted to appear clever, interesting, and intelligent, the last thing I wanted to do was talk too much. "Boys appreciate a good listener. They don't want someone droning on about her friends and her family the whole time. They want someone who wants to hear what they have to say. Ask questions," the article advised. "Show an interest in him and the things he likes. Don't be overly critical. If he likes to dip his french fries in his milk shake and this makes you feel sick, don't shout out that it's the grossest thing you've ever seen. Make a joke of it. If you can't make a joke, just ignore it."

The bath got cold. I poured in some more oil and added hot water.

"On the other hand," the article continued, "boys don't want to go out with a mindless robot. Don't smile too much or laugh too loudly at his jokes, he'll think you're insincere. If you disagree with something he says, don't start to argue, think about it and consider his point of view. Selfishness has no role in any relationship. Let him know that you're a person who knows how to give as well as receive; show him you know how to compromise. Don't be too serious. Boys like girls who can make them laugh."

I put in more oil and more hot water.

To put yourself at ease, the article suggested that you think about the things you did or said unconsciously that someone who didn't know you might well find annoying. Did you eat with your mouth open? Did you talk while you were eating? Did you slurp? Did you bite your nails? Chew your hair? Toss your head all the time? Stick out your tongue when you laughed? Say "you know" or "well" or "right" or "cool" every sentence or two?

By the time I got out of the bath, my skin was so shrivelled I looked like a large pink raisin. I used some of the skin cream my grandmother had given my mother to go with the bath oil, and then I studied myself carefully in the mirror. I practised laughing without showing my tonsils. I watched myself chew. I watched myself walk. I counted how many times a minute I blinked. I decided to gel my hair.

I was too nervous and excited for supper. I pushed my food around my plate a few times, and then I excused myself and went to get dressed.

I was ready by six-thirty. I studied myself in the mirror again. I looked all right. As long as I remembered to keep my mouth shut when I smiled, so he couldn't see my broken tooth, and I didn't grind my teeth out of nervousness, I would be OK.

"This is it!" I told my reflection. "The beginning of my destiny! The beginning of romance and love."

My reflection gazed back at me. *Or maybe not,* it seemed to be saying. I'd been so busy worrying about what I was going to wear that I hadn't thought of all the things that could go wrong. Maybe it wouldn't be the beginning of my destiny. Maybe it would be the beginning of the end.

I paced back and forth in my room, checking the clock every three minutes, thinking of all the things that could go wrong. There were quite a few.

What if he was late and by the time he arrived I was all damp and sweaty from anxiety, and in a bad mood? What if I suddenly came down with a cold and coughed and sneezed through the entire game? What if the basketball game was as boring as I'd always thought it would be?

Then there was our house to worry about. He hadn't been inside yet. Nothing was co-ordinated. The walls were covered with posters and photographs and anything else that couldn't fit on a shelf. Bill's house looked like a photograph in some magazine like *House and Garden,* but ours looked like a junk shop.

And there was my mother to worry about, too. She wasn't elegant and sophisticated like Bill's mother. What if Bill made some joke about her being a plumber and she gave him one of her twenty-minute lectures on job equality? Or, worse still, what if he told her we'd been to McDonald's? Then he'd get her half-hour lecture on the greed of multinational companies.

And that wasn't all I had to worry about, either. There was family history as well. My mother's first date with my father had been a total disaster. I was afraid that I might have inherited a gene from my parents that destroyed relationships before they began.

I started chanting to myself as I paced. First I chanted his name ... *Bill ... Bill ... Bill.* Then I chanted all the things we had in common ... no watch ... purple...

At one minute to seven I stopped. At exactly

seven the doorbell rang. I was just closing the door of my room behind me. My mother was already at the entrance to the living-room. Normally she slouched around the house in her old jeans and T-shirts that were either tie-dyed or said things like "Help the Earth Fight Back" or "Hands Off Central America" with her hair all over the place, but tonight she had her hair kind of tied back and she was wearing a red floral dress that was actually becoming. She didn't even look like a plumber. She looked almost normal. I'd forgotten she said she was going out. I stopped where I was. I didn't want Bill to think I'd been waiting anxiously or anything. I heard my mother say, "You must be Bill." And then she called out, "Mike! Mike, Bill's here."

I counted to ten and then I very slowly and casually strolled into the living-room. I can't say that he looked particularly awestruck when he saw me. In fact, I don't think he noticed me till I was practically on top of them. He was busy telling my mother all about his jeep. Much to my surprise, she was acting as though she were actually interested.

But I was struck by Bill. The moment I saw him I went into cardiac arrest. He was wearing beige chinos and a heavy green shirt and a blue knit tie. I'd never seen a boy wearing a tie unless he was at a wedding or something like that. It seemed really grown-up. He looked more perfect than ever. I pinched myself to make sure it wasn't just another dream. It didn't seem possible that he could be going out with me.

"Hi," said Bill. He pulled a single red rose from behind his back and handed it to me. "For you."

I made a joke so he wouldn't notice how I was blushing. "You're pretty punctual for someone who doesn't wear a watch."

Bill winked. "There's a clock on my mobile."

"You know, I can recommend a good mechanic if you ever need one," said my mother. "Plus, he's honest."

Bill whipped a small leather-bound address book from his jacket pocket. "Let me have it," he said, laughing.

My mother gave him John's name and phone number.

When Bill had finished writing, I said, "Well, I guess we better get going. We don't want to be late for the game."

"Have a nice time," said my mother. "I have to do something about my face," and she disappeared towards the bathroom. I took this as a sign. My mother wasn't going to hassle him about how long he'd had his licence or what time he was going to bring me back. Fate was in my corner. Everything was going to be all right.

"How come your mother called you Mike?" asked Bill as he opened the door of the jeep for me.

If anybody else had asked me that, I'd have said, "Because it's my name," but I didn't want Bill to think I was the sarcastic type. "It's just her nickname for me," I answered. "You know, from when I was little."

"Well, I'm not calling you by a boy's name," said Bill. He smiled. "After all, you're not little any more, are you?"

No, I'm not, I thought. I'm not little any more. I was about to meet my destiny.

AND THEN HE
KISSED ME

I'll remember that night for as long as I live. I felt like I'd been transported to a parallel world. It looked pretty much like the world I was used to – you know, same roads, same trees, same people, same houses – but it was about a hundred times better. A million times more intense. Everything was bright and shining, even in the dark. Bright and shining and vibrating with energy.

All the way to the game I watched me and Bill driving along as though I were watching a movie. I wanted to make sure I wasn't tossing my head or laughing too loudly or anything like that, but I also wanted to remember every second of that night; every subatomic detail. *After all*, I thought, *this might be the night I fall in love*.

We talked all the way while the radio played and the engine rumbled and the stars flickered in the sky like distant candles. At least Bill talked. I was too busy trying to watch us and remember the things I'd planned to say and not do anything wrong. It took an awful lot of concentration.

Bill told me what TV shows he liked. I hadn't seen any of them. My mother discouraged too much television. She said it was like doing nothing, accompanied by pictures and sound. But I didn't say that to Bill. I didn't want him to think I was any weirder than he already did.

"What about you?" he asked when he was through.

"Oh, me?" I said breezily. "I mainly watch nature documentaries. You know, 'A Day in the Life of a Lizard' – that kind of thing."

Bill laughed. "You're pretty funny, aren't you?" he asked.

About a zillion electrons zipped through me. He thought I was funny! Bone always said that the most important thing about a person was that she had a good sense of humour. I agreed.

Bill glanced over with a grin. "Come on," he coaxed. "What do you really watch?"

"Old films," I said quickly. I didn't want him to realize I hadn't been joking. Then he would think I was weird. Weird and not funny. "I really love Hitchcock—"

"*Psycho*," cut in Bill. "That's a great movie."

Then he told me what music he liked. I didn't listen to the radio much, but when I did I listened to classic rock or the jazz and blues station.

"I can't believe you've never heard Nirvana," said Bill. "Everybody I know is into them."

"Oh, I've heard them," I said quickly. "But I guess I never really listened."

Bill slipped a tape into the cassette player. "You should," he said. "I bet you'd like them. They're intense."

It wasn't the kind of music I'd ever wanted to really listen to before, but I could see that Bill was right. I should give it a chance. How could I be sure I didn't like it when I'd never really heard it?

"If you want, I'll lend you a tape so you can listen at home," he said.

A few zillion more electrons shot through my body. He took it for granted that he'd see me again. He knew we were destined to fall in love.

"I'd really like that," I said.

Bill told me about college. He didn't see why he had to take courses he wasn't interested in, like English and history and science. He didn't mind having to take maths because that was useful if you planned to run a chain of Parisian bistros, but what use were English, history and science to him?

I hadn't thought of it like that before. I'd always figured anything you learned was useful in one way or another. Bone called it opening your options. But I didn't say so to Bill.

"It isn't like I have to have read James Joyce in order to make a projection graph, is it?" he asked.

I thought about it for a few seconds. "I can see your point," I said at last.

He asked me about school and I told him it was OK.

Bill shook his head. "God." He laughed. "When I think of some of the things Mark and I used to do when we were in high school…" They cut classes. They put a duck in the boys' shower room. They Super Glued the principal's chair to the floor.

I'd known he must have had a rebellious streak. Like Henry Fonda in *Mister Roberts*. I laughed so much I nearly stopped breathing.

"Maybe we'll have time after the game to go to this little café I know," Bill said as he parked. He gave me a smile. "You'll like it."

He already knew me; already knew what I'd like. I floated out of the jeep. I was destiny's child.

The arena was packed by the time we arrived.

"Jeez," I said as I followed Bill in. "It looks like half of Santa Clara's here."

Bill waved to someone on the left side of the

room. "Don't worry," he said. "My friends are saving us seats."

Disappointment hit me like a sledgehammer. It hadn't occurred to me that we would be watching the game with Bill's friends. I thought we were going to be alone. Well, as alone as you can get in a crowd of three thousand. I pictured me and Bill sitting close together: he leaned even closer to explain the game to me; he put his arm around my shoulder to point out something that was happening on the court…

By the time I started moving again, Bill was already at the bleachers. He looked back at me. "Come on," he called. He pointed towards the top, where a couple was already shifting over to make room for us. They looked old. I wondered if maybe I should start wearing make-up.

I came on, trying not to step on anyone as I climbed up after Bill.

Bill's friends were Hal and his girlfriend, Layla. Hal was large and blond and pretty ordinary looking. He didn't have any of Bill's style. Layla was small and blonde and pretty in a kind of obvious way. Hal and Layla must have known Bill was bringing me if they were saving us seats, but they didn't act like they did. I caught them glancing at each other while Bill introduced us, as though they were asking, "Who's this?"

Hal said, "Hi," and started talking to Bill.

Layla leaned around Hal, said, "Hi," and started listening to Hal talk to Bill.

I can admit it. I probably wouldn't have liked the game if I hadn't been with Bill. If I'd been with Bone and Hope, for example, I would have spent the whole time goofing around. If I'd been with Hal and Layla by myself, I would have passed out with boredom before half-time.

But I was with Bill. Because he and Hal were pretty involved in the game even before it started, I didn't have a chance to admit to him that I hadn't seen all that many basketball games before. So he didn't lean close to me while he explained what was happening. I didn't care. His body rubbed against mine every time he moved. His voice was in my ear whenever he shouted something to the players. It was my feet he stepped on whenever Santa Clara came even close to making a basket and he leaped up, shouting. The first time he got to his feet like that it made me feel a little embarrassed. I could imagine Bone's reaction if he'd been there. But Bone wasn't there, and a lot of the people who were, were getting to their feet, too. I stopped thinking about what Bone would say. By half-time I was jumping to my feet and shouting with everyone else.

Hal and Layla wanted to go for pizza after the

game. I didn't want to go for pizza. I wanted to go to the little café that Bill knew. This was our first date; I wanted to be just with Bill. But in all the excitement of the game I guess he forgot about the café. Because instead of saying we had other plans, Bill said, "That sounds great." He turned to me. "What do you think, Michelle? You up for pizza?"

I remembered what the magazine article had said about not being critical. But I also remembered what it had said about not being a robot. "Is that the café you were telling me about?" I asked innocently.

Bill's smile vanished. He had forgotten. "The café!" He turned to Hal and Layla. "I promised Michelle I'd take her to Delancy's."

"But we always get pizza after the game," Hal protested.

"You can take her another time," said Layla. She gave me a smile.

Bill looked from them to me. He was torn. "Would you mind if we didn't go to the café tonight?" He leaned a little closer. "It's just that it's kind of a tradition," he added softly.

I couldn't say I minded. And, besides, I didn't really any more. He'd asked me if I minded if we didn't go "tonight". That meant he was still planning to take me. It was practically another date. "Of course not," I said quickly. "Pizza would be great."

*   *   *

We sat in a booth at the back. Layla sat next to me and Hal sat next to Bill.

I picked up one of the menus the waiter had brought us with our water. I looked at the others. None of them had taken a menu. Bill and Hal were still laughing about some friend of theirs who had accidentally shot in the other team's basket. Layla was searching through her bag for an emery board.

"Let's just get the usual," said Hal.

"Sounds good to me," said Bill.

Layla said she didn't care.

I put my unopened menu back on the table. *The usual* ... it made it sound as though the four of us always went out together. "That sounds good to me, too," I said.

Bill caught the waiter's attention as he was walking by. "We'll have the usual," he informed him. "And four large Pepsis."

The waiter nodded. "Not too much ice, right?"

I figured that they must have eaten here before.

"Now that the weather's getting better we should go out on the boat," said Layla. She turned to me. "We had some of the best times last summer."

Bill laughed. "Remember the time we went to Marita?"

Layla started laughing, too. "You mean the time Hal nearly drowned us all?"

149

"It was practically a monsoon," roared Hal. "You can't hold me responsible for what happens in a monsoon."

"Oh, yes we can." Bill pretended to tremble. "I still have nightmares about that rock suddenly looming at us out of the rain."

"Gee," I said. "That must have been scary."

"We should plan a barbecue at the cove," said Layla. "Spend a whole day."

"I love barbecues, too," I said. "But we usually have them in the backyard."

"We've had some of the greatest beach parties in the history of the world there," Bill was saying. "I remember this one time…" He turned back to Layla and Hal. "You remember Barbara's barbecue?"

Hal started choking with laughter. "That was the best, man," he gasped. "That was absolutely the best…"

Mara, Jamie, Steve, Justin, Eva, and someone named Archie, who barfed in the cooler, had all been there. Hal cracked us all up with the story of the barbecued beach-ball. Even though I didn't know any of the people they were talking about, I didn't really mind. It wouldn't be long before I did know them, before I was part of the gang that went to the cove.

"It sounds great," I said. "I wish I'd been there."

"We really should make some plans," said Layla.

150

"Yeah, sure," said Bill. "We should go again soon."

Hal pointed over my head. "Food!" he roared. I glanced round. Our waiter was weaving his way between the tables with an enormous silver tray in his hands. "It's about time," said Hal. "I'm starving."

"Smell it!" said Bill as the waiter stopped beside our booth. "My mouth is watering already."

The waiter slid the pie on to our table. The smell of it made me catch my breath. "The usual" was an extra large pizza, half meatballs and half pepperoni. I guess I'd figured that since Bill had given it his OK it must be mushroom or pepper. He'd teased me about being a vegetarian when we were in McDonald's. He couldn't have forgotten.

"But I can't eat that!" I was so astounded that I just blurted it out.

Hal looked at me as though I'd thrown up on the table or something.

"Allergy?" asked Layla.

Bill groaned. "Oh, Michelle, I'm sorry. I really am." He looked at the others. "Michelle's a veggie," he explained.

"You mean she doesn't eat meat?" asked Hal. "What does she eat if she doesn't eat meat?"

Bill gave a little shrug. "Vegetables."

Hal laughed. "Maybe she should have

ordered a bowl of lettuce."

"Maybe you should have ordered a bunch of bananas," I muttered under my breath.

Layla heard me. "Don't pay any attention to them," she advised. "They're jocks. Bill's been changing his image since he started working at the restaurant, but he's still a jock underneath. They don't think they've been fed if they haven't had at least half a cow." She gave me a conspiratorial smile. "I understand. You're on a diet, aren't you? I almost went veggie myself once." She laughed. "I mean, how many calories can there be in a carrot?"

Bill turned to me with a sad face. "Do you want me to order you a small cheese or something?" he asked. "Or can you just scrape it off?"

I couldn't look into those eyes and stay upset. And, anyway, what did it matter? "It's all right," I said. "Of course I can just scrape it off."

We talked all the way home, though I couldn't really say about what. Everything, I guess. What I do remember is that it was a clear and starry night, and the mountain road was lit by moonlight like the road in a fairy tale.

My mother's van was back in the driveway when we pulled up, but the house was dark.

Bill and I sat in the jeep and talked some more.

Eventually we got around to Hal and Layla. Bill said Hal wouldn't have teased me if he hadn't thought I was cool. "Layla really likes you, too," he said. "I think she was surprised by you."

"You mean because I'm a vegetarian?" I joked.

Bill grinned. "No, it was Hal who was surprised by that." He gave an embarrassed laugh. "You know, because you're still in high school. She wasn't expecting you to be so—" He stared at me, still grinning.

"So what?" I prompted.

He laughed again. "So you. She said we look really good together."

What about you, I silently asked. *What do you think?*

It was like he read my mind. "And I think so, too," he whispered.

We sat there in the moonlight shining through the windshield, smiling at each other.

"So do I," I whispered back.

Bill put a hand on my shoulder.

And then he kissed me.

That was the moment when I fell in love.

"I'm in love," I announced to Leonardo. Just saying the words made me feel happier than I'd ever felt before. Leonardo wasn't my first choice as a confidant, but I had to tell someone and Hope wasn't home. Her mother said

153

she'd gone out with Bone. I was relieved to hear that – I didn't want to think of her sitting by herself while I was out falling in love.

"I'm in love... I'm in love," I said over and over. No wonder there were so many songs about it. There was nothing else like it in the universe. I felt as though I'd died and gone to heaven. I'd heard that phrase at least a zillion times – mainly from my grandmother – but I'd never known what it meant. Until now. My life was complete. There was nothing else to want.

I lifted Leonardo into the air. "I am really and truly in love," I told him.

Leonardo looked back at me silently.

"It's incredible," I continued. "It's absolutely the biggest thrill there is."

Leonardo poohed on my lap. I put him back in his vivarium and went to the kitchen for a paper towel.

I tiptoed into the kitchen. My mother was already asleep and I didn't want to wake her. If she came out, I knew I'd wind up telling her I was in love – I was too excited not to. I couldn't stop thinking about Bill. I wanted to see him again right away. I put my hand to my lips; they were still warm from his kiss. But if I told my mother I was in love she'd manage to shoot me down. "In love?" she'd shriek. "After one date? What are you going to do on your third date, get divorced?"

I was just going back to my room when I thought I heard a car pull up outside. I froze, waiting to see what would happen next. It was times like that when I could see the advantage of having a killer dog like Gringo and not a tortoise.

I held my breath and listened. Footsteps were coming up the steps to the porch. Someone was trying the door. For a nanosecond I actually stopped thinking about Bill. But then I realized who it was. Bill! It had to be Bill! He couldn't stop thinking about me, either. He wanted to see me again right away, too. He was trying to catch my attention without waking my mom. I could still feel the touch of his mouth on mine. I wanted him to kiss me again. If I'd had the nerve – and a car – I would have gone straight to his house and stood in the moonlight, throwing stones against his bedroom window. Why shouldn't he feel the same?

The door swung open suddenly. I was so sure it was going to be Bill that it took me a second to realize that the person stepping into the living-room was my mother. John must have picked her up and driven her home.

"Why are you looking at me like that?" she demanded.

"Like what?"

"Like you forgot that I live here," said my mother.

LOVE IS ALL
THAT MATTERS

Hope called me first thing Saturday morning. She apologized for not being in when I phoned, but Bone had seemed depressed so she'd agreed to hang out with him. He'd gone through every album he had that had a fiddle on it, while they played Scrabble. Bone won, 421 to 219, and convinced Hope to borrow one of his Eddie Lejeune tapes. She asked me how my date had gone.

"We had the best time," I told her. "It's really, really incredible, Hope, but it's like we're two parts of the same whole."

"Twin souls," breathed Hope. "Separated by birth ... united by love."

I had the feeling she was quoting from some old movie poster, but it sounded right. Twin souls, brought together by Fate.

It wasn't easy keeping my voice down. "Cel-Ray soda," I went on in a rush. "Can you believe it? I thought you and me and Bone were practically the only people in California who had even heard of Cel-Ray soda, but not only has Bill heard of it, he likes it as much as I do."

"Jeez," said Hope. "It is incredible. I mean, what are the chances of a coincidence like that?"

"About two zillion to one. But that's not all, Hope. Guess what. Guess who his dentist is. Dr Everett! Can you believe it? It's amazing I've never run into him in the waiting room. And he broke his arm when he was nine, just like I did. The same arm, Hope. Only he didn't fall out of a tree, he was hit by a bat. And he always eats apple pie with cheddar cheese. And he loves *Psycho*. And he has a scar on his index finger. And he puts mayonnaise on his fries, not ketchup."

Hope laughed. "And you thought you didn't have a chance. I told you to trust Fate."

"I'll never doubt your advice again," I said.

She asked me what we did after the game, and I told her about going for pizza with Hal and Layla.

"Wow, hanging out with the college crowd," said Hope in mock awe. "So tell me. What are his friends like?"

"Oh, you know," I said. "He's a jock and she's really into make-up and clothes, but they're really nice."

"I'm surprised they're friends of Bill's," said Hope. "They don't sound much like him."

"Oh, they're nothing like him," I said quickly. "I think he just hangs out with them because he and Hal went to high school together. And Layla said Bill's been changing his image lately."

"I bet that's why he likes you," said Hope. "Because you're different."

Hope wanted me to go baby-sitting with her that afternoon and then stay over at her place so we wouldn't miss our weekly video night after all, but I explained that I couldn't. "I can't leave the house," I told her. "Bill might call." It was the last thing he'd said: I'll call you.

"Why don't I come over after I'm done baby-sitting," Hope suggested. "I'll pick up the videos on the way."

I wanted to say yes, but I was afraid to. What if Bill did call and wanted me to go out with him that night? If I turned him down he might not ask me again.

I sighed regretfully. "I really should work on my English paper." Which was true. I really should. Since I couldn't think of anything else, I'd decided to go with my mother's idea. I was going to compare *Romeo and Juliet* with *When Harry Met Sally* to show the difference between old-fashioned true love and modern unemotional practicality. So far, I hadn't gotten any further than putting the title on the page: "Old Coats and Bolts of Lightning." "It's due in a few weeks and I haven't even started it yet."

"Oh. Right," said Hope. "Well, let me know if you change your mind. You know, if you get a lot done on it this afternoon."

"I will," I promised. If Bill didn't call by five, it was pretty unlikely that I'd be going out with him that night. "I'll see how it goes."

I stayed in my room all morning. I put on Bill's favourite radio station. It wasn't a station I ever listened to, but I'd promised him I'd try it. "Compliments on Your Kiss" was playing. I picked up the refrain right away. *Every time I think of you I wish,*" I sang. I wondered if Bill was listening, too. I wondered if he was singing along.

I lay on my bed, going over every second of the night before, especially that last second – the one when he kissed me. Bill's kiss had been as soft and gentle as being smushed by a marshmallow. If I closed my eyes I could still feel his lips on mine. Meltdown. I figured I'd probably never wash my mouth again. If I could've come up with a way to drink without getting my lips wet, I would have.

When I wasn't reliving his kiss, I was imagining reasons why he hadn't called me yet: He'd woken up late because he'd found it hard to get to sleep last night. He'd had to go to work and hadn't had a chance to get to a phone. He couldn't find my number, and he wouldn't be able to look it up in the directory because my mother used her maiden name and I'd forgotten to tell him what it was.

At about eleven-thirty, I went to make sure that the receiver hadn't been knocked off the hook or something. My mother was sitting at the table with the phone cord stretched halfway across the kitchen, talking. There was an empty coffee cup in front of her. No wonder Bill hadn't called. She looked as though she'd been there for ages.

She seemed as surprised to see me as I'd been to see her last night. "It's Mike," she said into the mouthpiece. "I thought you'd gone out," she said to me.

Just how long had she been on the phone? How long was she planning to stay on?

"Who is it?" I whispered. If it was my grandmother she could be there for a couple more hours.

"It's John." She laughed at something he said and started talking again.

I went back to my room.

"When Will I See You Again?" was playing on the radio. This was a song I'd heard a few hundred times before, but I'd never really listened to the words. I'd just thought it was a catchy tune. Now, however, I understood the anguish and pain the singer was feeling. I took my ticket stub from the basketball game out of my wallet. I started singing along.

I spent about a half-hour sticking the ticket into the frame of my mirror. Then I went back to the kitchen.

I couldn't believe it. My mother was still on the phone.

My mother put her hand over the mouthpiece. "Now what?" she asked. "Why are you hovering?"

"Nothing," I answered. "It's just that I'm expecting a call."

If I'd thought the fact that I was waiting for a call while she was chatting away would make her feel guilty about staying on the phone, I'd been wrong.

"So?" said my mother. "He'll call back." I didn't say anything, I was trying to will her to realize that she was ruining my life. It didn't work. "Why don't you go out?" she continued. "It's a beautiful day."

I didn't move. "I can't. I have to work on my English paper."

"So go work on it," said my mother.

I went back to my room.

I got out my books, my notes, and a pad of paper and a pen. I put them on my desk. I sat down at my desk. But I couldn't concentrate on my English paper. Bill's face floated above the lined page. *Things can only get better,* sang the radio. I started to sing along. It's true, I thought. Things can only get better. I've met

161

the boy of my dreams, everything's downhill from now on.

By five o'clock I had a wastebasket filled with crumpled sheets of paper. I'd written the title of my paper on a few of them, and on one or two I'd actually written the first sentence as well. But aside from that, they were covered with stuff like M & B ... B.C. FOR EVER ... BILL & MICHELLE...

I thought of phoning Hope to tell her to come over, but then I decided that it was still a little early. If Bill had to work, he'd probably just be quitting about now. I had to give him time to get home and change. He might call me after that.

I didn't call Hope at six, either, because I thought I might have been wrong about what time Bill got off work. He'd explained how they rotated shifts, but he'd also said that he often worked later than he was supposed to. It was all part of his management training.

At seven I went into the kitchen to see if my mother was fixing supper. I wasn't really hungry but I needed something to do.

My mother wasn't fixing supper. "John and I are going out for Mexican," she informed me. "We thought it might be nice if you came along."

"I can't," I said. "I want to finish my paper."

"Even Shakespeare took a break now and

then," said my mother.

Not when he was in love, he hadn't.

As soon as my mother left, I went to the phone. Even if she didn't feel like coming over any more, I needed to talk to Hope. I dialled her number. I hung up on the first ring. If Hope and I started talking now, Bill wouldn't get through for hours.

At eight I called the phone company to have them check the line. Maybe there was something wrong. Maybe we weren't receiving incoming calls.

At nine I gave up and called Hope.

"Bobby's come over to teach me a couple of songs," said Hope. "Why don't you hang out with us?"

This surprised me. "I thought Bone had his band today." Bone was usually incapable of speech, never mind movement, after spending a day with the band.

"He did have the band," said Hope. "And now he's here."

"It must have gone pretty well," I suggested. He'd never been in the mood to hang out with me afterwards.

Hope moved her mouth away from the receiver. "I'll be there in a second," she shouted. "So why don't you come over?" she said to me. She lowered her voice. "Leave the machine on in case Bill calls."

The mention of Bill drove Bone from my

163

mind. What if Bill didn't like answering machines? What if he didn't leave a message? What if he thought I was screening my calls?

"I can't," I said. "I'm almost done with my first draft. I might as well get it over with." Someone started screaming in the background.

"I've got to go," said Hope. "Bone's blown a fuse plugging in his amp."

After she hung up, I sat on the sofa and just stared at the blank TV screen for a while. Maybe I should have gone with my mom and John. Maybe I should go over to Hope's, after all.

I was just about to reach for the phone to call Hope back when it rang.

"You don't have call waiting, do you, Michelle?" asked Bill.

He'd been trying to get me all day, just as I'd known that he was. He'd really had a good time the night before. He'd been thinking about me a lot. He was sorry to call so late on a Saturday – he'd been sure I'd be out – but he'd been in the restaurant since six and this was the first chance he'd had to try me again.

"I know you're probably busy," said Bill, "but I was wondering if you wanted to go sailing tomorrow. I don't have to be at work until seven."

I couldn't answer. I was seeing Bill and me drifting on an ocean like glass, holding hands as we watched the clouds move above us. Even though we were miles from anyone we were talking softly. We didn't want to disturb the fish. We didn't want to drown the singing of the wind. Our shoulders just touching, our eyes on the distant horizon, we opened up our hearts, we shared the secrets of our souls. *I've never told anyone this before,* Bill whispered. I gently pushed a lock of hair from his eyes. *Me neither,* I sighed. *I can only tell you,* whispered Bill. *And I can only tell you...*

Bill cleared his throat. "I guess you're busy, huh?"

In the back of my mind was the thought that I *was* busy on Sunday, but I pushed it away. Whatever it was, it couldn't be as important as this.

"No," I said quickly. "No, I'm not busy."

"Great," said Bill. "I'll pick you up at one."

My mother and John were fixing brunch when I got up the next morning. I was beginning to think that John lived in our kitchen.

"You should have come with us last night," said John. "Carol and I have discovered the best Mexican diner this side of the border."

"John and I are going to drive up the coast this afternoon," said my mother. "Why don't you come along?"

I stuck my head in the fridge, in case my face gave away how excited I was. "I can't." I kept my voice casual as I studied the contents of the top shelf. "I have a date."

John looked up from beating the eggs. "Bring Bone along," he said. "I'd like to hear what he thinks of the new sound system I've rigged up in the car."

My eyes moved to the second shelf. "Not with Bone," I began.

"Mike's got a new boyfriend," said my mother.

I pulled my head out so fast I banged it on the door. "Bone has never been my boyfriend," I informed her coolly. "We've never been anything more than friends."

My mother looked at John; John looked at my mother. They exchanged a smile.

"Well, we haven't," I said, a little less coolly.

"This one's name is Bill," said my mother. She was still looking at John. "He works in that new restaurant in Spoon Falls."

I regained my cool. "Actually, his father owns Chez Moi."

"Oh, right." John nodded. He was still looking at my mother. "The Parisian bistro in the middle of the redwoods."

"It happens to be a very good restaurant," I said a little sharply. It was bad enough living with a cynic without having one visit as well.

John gave me a wink. "So, am I going to meet this Bill?"

"He's not picking me up till later," I said quickly. And then, in case they'd forgotten they had plans, I added, "I thought you two were going for a drive."

"Ooh," said my mother. "I can tell when I'm not wanted."

John grinned in my direction. "He better be worth missing a great black-bean burrito for," he said.

"There she is," said Bill, pointing proudly to the sleek white sailboat. "*Meadowlark I.*"

I'd never given boats much thought before, but even I could see that this one was special. It probably cost as much as our house. "She's beautiful," I said admiringly.

"Twenty-six-foot fibreglass body, main cylinder jib, sleeps two," said Bill. He held out his hands to help me aboard.

"She's really beautiful." I put my hands on his shoulders and got ready to float into his arms. The sunlight brought out the dark blue flecks of colour in his eyes.

Bill stepped back to swing me to the deck. Nothing happened for a second. I didn't glide through the air as I'd expected, I didn't find my body pressed against Bill's as he gently set me down. I stayed where I was, balanced between the dock and the edge of the boat, as though an invisible hand were holding me back. The long white scarf I'd worn to match the romance of the occasion had gotten caught on the mooring. I gave it a tug. Bill looked like he was about to say something – something like, "What are you doing?" – when there was a sudden ripping sound. I crashed into Bill. Bill crashed to the floor with a scream of pain.

Bill said he wasn't really hurt. He'd just lost his wind when he hit the deck. He said that if you were going to have an accident it was just as well to have it before you'd left the land. He sat me down and told me not to move. Then he got us out of the harbour without any more trouble.

"I thought maybe we'd go to the famous cove," said Bill as we glided away from the yacht club.

At the risk of looking less than perfect, I screwed my eyes up so I could see him, even though the sun was in my face.

He smiled at me over his shoulder. "I'd like you to see it." He winked. "It's a great place, even if you're not having a barbecue."

I smiled back. This was even better than I'd hoped. Bill was taking me to the cove so we could be alone in a romantic setting. I stuffed my torn scarf into my pocket. "I'd love to go," I said softly.

Bill motioned me to sit beside him. "Come here," he said. "I'll teach you how to sail."

I didn't need to be asked again. I went and sat beside him. It was like sitting in front of a fire.

If we'd been sucked into the sea right then, I wouldn't have cared. At least I'd die happy.

Bill explained that because we were sailing against the wind we'd have to tack. This meant going up at an angle and coming back down.

"The tricky part is when we change direction," Bill went on. "When the sails are right out, the boom will swing across." He gave me another of his mega-grins. "Don't forget to duck."

I didn't forget to duck. I just didn't do it fast enough.

"Get down!" screamed Bill.

I flung myself to the deck as the boom swung over my head. The floor was wet. I scraped my cheek.

"There's a towel and a first aid kit in the cabin," said Bill. "You take the tiller and I'll go get them."

I didn't want to take the tiller. I didn't want the boom to attack me again. "You stay there," I said. "I'll get them. Just tell me where they are."

Bill started telling me where to find the towel and the first aid kit. I opened the cabin door.

"Oh, no," Bill shouted as something small and brown and white hurled itself into my arms. "I forgot about him."

Gringo sat beside Bill all the rest of the way. Whenever I got too close to them, Gringo growled. "He thinks you don't like him," said Bill.

"I think he doesn't like me," I said.

Bill gave me a wink. "Well, I like you," he said.

"Likewise," I said.

Gringo bared his teeth.

In the end, we never made it to the cove. The combination of the wind and trying to keep me and Gringo apart defeated even Bill's sailing skills. Instead, he pulled in the sheets and let her drift while the clouds slid overhead and sunshine glowed on the water like lights. There was no sound but the beating of my heart, the low but steady grumble of Gringo as he leaned against Bill, his eyes on me, and the murmur of Bill's voice as he talked about his dreams.

He wanted to make a million dollars by the time he was thirty.

"Really?" I was impressed. Even if it had occurred to me to want a million dollars, it would never have occurred to me to plan so far in advance.

"You have to know what you want out of life," Bill told me. "That way you know what you're aiming for." He also wanted a Porsche, a house on the ocean, and his own basketball court. He asked me what I wanted.

"I want a Jackson's chameleon or an iguana," I answered immediately. It was the best I could do for long-term goals.

Bill laughed. "No, really, what do you want?"

I said I was interested in working in the movies.

"Just think." Bill grinned, squeezing my hand. "I may be sitting next to the next Julia Roberts."

I didn't have the heart to tell him I didn't mean that I wanted to be an actress. I was too happy. I don't think I'd ever felt so happy in my life. Yesterday I'd thought I was in love; but now I knew it. I squeezed his hand back. I sighed with joy. It was as though we were the only two people in a still and perfect world. The only two people and their vicious bull terrier.

Bill had to go straight to work after he brought me home, so we said goodbye at the car. When I was little I couldn't understand what the big deal was about kissing. The thought of mashing my lips against someone else's didn't really strike me as a lot of fun. Plus there were the germs and the saliva to consider. I figured the saliva was the worst. This guy in a truck spat on our windshield once when we were stuck in traffic, and I nearly threw up. I just knew I'd gag if someone started spitting in my mouth. But Bill's kiss wasn't revolting at all. It was like being drawn into the sky. This time when he kissed me, I kissed him back. Gringo started throwing himself against the window of the jeep. But I didn't care. He could chew his way through the glass, he wasn't going to stop our kiss. Mrs Iler next door came out of her house. I didn't care. I didn't care if the whole street saw us. I hoped they did. I felt like Juliet. I could hear the neighbours phoning one another up. "Did you see Mike Brindisi?" they'd ask. "She was standing in the driveway. Kissing a boy!" "Not 'a boy'," I would tell them. "*The* boy." We stopped kissing when Gringo set off the horn.

I didn't remember what it was I was supposed to do that day until I got in the house. And then I only remembered because my mother told me. When Bone gave me the ride to the mall, I'd promised him I'd go listen to his new B.B. King album.

"There were three messages on the machine from Hope," said my mother as soon as I walked through the door. "She's at Bobby's." She looked at me again. "What happened to you?"

"I'm happy," I told her. Which was actually an understatement. I was practically glowing with love.

"I meant to your face," said my mother. "It looks like it's been bleeding."

I called Hope, but she wasn't home yet. I

didn't feel like calling her at Bone's. I knew Bone was going to be all worked up because I'd forgotten our date. I called Hope again after supper, but she was taking a bath.

Before I could try once more, Bill phoned me. It was a slow night at Chez Moi. He was taking a break in the office. Bill said that slow nights were worse than really busy ones because there was nothing to do. He said that once they were so busy they'd run out of barbecue sauce and he'd had to make some with ketchup and Coca-Cola. I said I would never have thought of that in a million years. Bill said you had to be resourceful if you wanted to run a restaurant.

The minute I hung up with Bill, the phone rang, but my mother snatched it out of my hand.

"That'll be for me," she said.

She talked for so long that I forgot about calling Hope, and I guess Hope forgot about calling me.

The first thing I said to Hope the next day was, "Hi." The second was, "I'm really really sorry about yesterday, Hope. I totally forgot we were supposed to go over to Bone's."

"Obviously," said Hope.

"Please don't be mad at me," I pleaded. "It's just that Bill called me Saturday night and asked me to go out with him ... and ... well, everything else just went out of my head."

"I wasn't mad," said Hope. "I was hurt." She made a face. "The least you could've done was call and say you weren't coming."

"I know," I agreed. "I should've called. But how could I, Hope? I didn't remember I had something to do."

"Well…" Hope sighed. "I guess if the boy I was in love with suddenly asked me out, I'd have forgotten about everything else, too."

I hugged her. "Then you're not mad at me?" I asked.

"I told you," said Hope. "I wasn't mad." She almost smiled. "But Bobby is."

Bone was definitely mad. And not at all understanding. Despite the fact that I apologized every time Mr Hunter turned his back, Bone refused to speak to me in English class. He walked out without waiting for me.

But if I thought that Bone not speaking to me was the worst that could happen, I was wrong. The worst was when Hope and I joined him in the cafeteria and he *stopped* refusing to speak to me.

"I thought we had a date," he said as I sat down. He was staring straight at me in this unemotional way. "Since when don't you keep dates with your friends?"

I scraped my chair in. "I said I was sorry." And I was sorry. The last thing I wanted was for Bone to be mad at me.

Bone acted the same as he had the other six times I'd apologized. He pretended he hadn't heard me. "You could've called us, Mike. That's all you had to do, just pick up the phone and say, 'Sorry, guys, something better's come along.'"

Hope gave him a look. "Oh, come on," she groaned. "Give her a break, will you?"

"It wasn't like that," I protested. "I just forgot, that's all. Don't you ever forget anything?"

He stared back at me. "Only things that aren't important."

I banged my fists on the table. "Look, I'm sorry. What else can I say? I didn't do it on purpose, Bone. I just forgot."

He sucked in his cheeks, thinking. It meant he was ready to forgive me.

"I'm really, really sorry," I went on. "It won't happen again. I promise."

He picked up his sandwich. "All right," he mumbled through a mouthful of bread and cheese. "I accept your apology." He took another bite. "So what'd you do instead of hearing my new album? Prince Charming take you to a ball?"

The mention of Bill immediately made me feel better. "No, we went sailing! Bill says that after a stressful week at the restaurant sailing really relaxes him."

Bone could arch one eyebrow better than

anyone else I'd ever known. "Sailing! No wonder you didn't want to come over to my house."

Hope blew her straw wrapper at him. "Cut it out, will you?" She turned to me. "You didn't tell me you went sailing yesterday."

I hadn't told her anything, really. I'd been too busy grovelling. But I wasn't grovelling any more. "Yeah," I nodded happily. "Bill has his own boat. You should see it, Hope. Bill says it's the best in its class." I leaned towards her. "Bill says I'm a natural sailor. He says all I need is a few lessons and I'll be as good as most of the girls at the sailing club. Bill says—"

Bone's hand shot out so suddenly I nearly dropped my juice. "I can't stand it," he snapped. "Give me your Walkman. I'm not eating my lunch listening to what Bill says."

Before, Bone had made me feel bad because I knew he was right and I was wrong. But now, I wasn't wrong. It was a free country, wasn't it? I was allowed to talk about Bill if I wanted. Now he was just being annoying. I slapped my Walkman into his hand.

"So where'd you go?" asked Hope.

I forgot about Bone. "He was going to take me to this secret cove he knows. Bill says no one ever goes there because the inlet's a little tricky, but he's such a terrific sailor—" I broke off because I'd heard the pretty unmistakable sound of a Walkman being slammed down on a cafeteria table.

"Have aliens from AM radio taken over your body or something?" Bone demanded. He was waving the headset in the air. "What is this junk you've got in here?"

This time it was my turn to give him a cold unemotional look. "It isn't junk." I raised my chin. "It's Nirvana."

"Nirvana?" Bone looked as though he were trying not to spit-laugh. "Since when are you into Nirvana?" He slapped his forehead. "Oh, wait a minute. Let me guess." He made his voice sweet and high. "Bill says Nirvana is great," he mimicked.

To my surprise, it was Hope who laughed.

"What's so funny?" I demanded.

Hope's face went blank. "Well, you know..." She glanced over at Bone. Bone smiled.

"Well?" I prodded.

Hope shrugged. "Well, you do say 'Bill says' a lot."

I couldn't understand her. Hope was in favour of love. She was happy about me and Bill. Why was she acting like this? "So?" I asked. "Is that some kind of crime?"

Bone turned his smile on me. "Only against nature," he said.

I smiled back. I didn't care what Hope and Bone thought. They could laugh at me all they wanted. I was in love, and that was all that mattered.

ADDICTED TO LOVE

For that entire week, Bill was the first thing I thought of when I woke up in the morning, and the last thing I thought about before I fell asleep at night. As far as I was concerned, any time without Bill was just time that I had to get through before I could see or talk to him again. As soon as school was over, I rushed home in case he might call or stop by. As soon as supper was over, I locked myself in my room so I could think about him.

My mother said love was a drug. She said I was in a trance.

"Earth calling Mike," John shouted. Now he was coming over for brunch on Saturdays, too. "Please come in."

I'd been gazing at the bowl of fruit salad in front of me, wondering if Bill was likely to want to do something that day. Tuesday he'd taken me to watch him and his buddies play basketball, and Friday night – our one-week anniversary – we'd gone to the SCU away game in the next county. But he hadn't said anything about today. He just said he'd call. I looked up. "Were you talking to me?" I asked.

John laughed. "I was trying to."

"Ignore her," advised my mother. "Love's turned her into a zombie."

I smiled at her tolerantly. Her jokes didn't make me mad, they made me happy. The fact that my mother had finally noticed must have meant I was even more in love than I'd thought. And that meant she was finally taking me seriously.

"Anyway," said John, "I was trying to find out how you wanted your eggs."

"I'll have them scrambled," said a voice behind me.

I turned around. Bone and Hope were standing outside the screen door.

"Hi, everybody," said Hope.

"Come on in," said my mother.

I hadn't even heard Bone's truck pull up, but I had to admit that I was glad to see them. It suddenly hit me that I'd been kind of missing them without knowing it. I figured they must have come over to see if I wanted to do something. I decided right then that if Bill was too busy to see me, I might go with them. It wasn't that I was tired of sitting in my room by myself – I really enjoyed it – but I figured I could probably do with a little sunshine. Bill really liked girls with tans.

Hope took the chair next to mine. "You have a good time last night?" she asked.

"It was great," I answered immediately. "We went to the game in—"

Bone sat down next to Hope. "Maybe you should cook Mike's eggs in the shape of a basketball," he said loudly to John. He gave me a look out of the corner of his eye and added, "Or should it be a heart?"

My good mood at seeing them vanished instantly. Maybe my mother's jokes didn't make me mad, but Bone's did. I knew he didn't take me seriously. I smiled sweetly. "Nobody asked you to come here, you know," I said even more sweetly.

John turned his back on us and started cracking eggs. "Well, actually," he said over his shoulder, "I invited Bobby over."

"That's right," Bone grinned. "John's going to show me how to adjust the clutch on the pickup."

I couldn't believe it! He hadn't come to see me. He'd come to see John! I looked from Bone to Hope. I expected her to jump in and say that she'd come with him so she could hang out with me, but she didn't say anything. "What about you?" I prompted.

"Bone's taking me to get some sheet music later," said Hope.

So she hadn't come for me, either. "Oh," I said. "I see."

Hope must have heard something in my voice. "Why don't you come, too?" she asked quickly. "We won't be long."

"I can't," I said equally quickly. Even if Bone hadn't given her a *What are you doing?* look, I would have known that she'd only just thought of asking me. "I already have plans."

"I told you she'd be busy," Bone said to Hope.

Hope ignored him. "What about later?" she wanted to know. "Why don't you give me a ring when you get back and maybe we can get together?"

"OK," I promised. "I'll see how it goes."

Bone smiled at me over a glass of juice. "So many basketball games and so little time," he said.

Everybody laughed except me.

John and my mother left right after Bone and Hope. "We won't ask you to come with us, since you're busy," said my mother. They were going rafting in the state park. I was tempted to tell her that I wasn't busy after all – it was already after noon and Bill hadn't called – but I didn't. I watched them drive off, and then I went to my room.

Maybe I was a little more tired of sitting by myself, thinking about Bill than I'd thought, because after a couple of hours I actually got out my English stuff and started to work on my paper.

I began with Juliet. I could identify with her. She knew right away that Romeo was her destiny. That he was more important than anything else. Without him, she was just half a person. Romeo made her complete. I could picture Juliet sitting in her lonely room, writing "Juliet loves Romeo" on the cover of her diary while she gazed out of the window, waiting for him to suddenly appear on her balcony. I could see the look of yearning in her eyes, count the tears on her cheeks. Every time something rustled outside she rushed to the window. "Romeo?" she'd whisper. "Romeo, is that you?" It was a lot like me and Bill.

Thinking about Juliet began to depress me a little, so I decided to move on to Sally. From what I could remember of the movie, when Sally met Harry, she didn't even like him very much. Even afterwards, when they became really good friends, Sally didn't realize that Harry was her destiny. She thought he was just someone to hang out with when she couldn't get a date.

I couldn't recall many of the details of the film, so I went into the living-room to watch our copy on video.

Juliet may have spent a lot of time waiting for Romeo, but Sally didn't have that problem with Harry. Sally and Harry were always hanging out together. That was practically all they did. They went shopping, they watched TV, they took walks, they went out to eat. Juliet and Romeo never argued, but Sally and Harry argued the entire time.

I tried to imagine Juliet and Romeo hanging out like Sally and Harry, but I failed. What would they talk about after they'd exhausted the topic of how much they loved each other? What would they do? Go for walks? I couldn't see Juliet slogging through the woods in her satin skirts. Go dancing? Dancing seemed a little frivolous for Romeo. Would they cook together? I wondered. Would they play cards? I tried to picture Juliet and Romeo at home in the evening, but nothing happened. They just sat there, gazing longingly into each other's eyes.

There was something about the scene when Harry helps Sally buy a Christmas tree that really got to me. It reminded me of Bone. When I wanted to build Leonardo's tank, Bone helped me design it. He went with me to get the materials. We dumped the lengths of chipboard and the acrylic sheets in the back of the pickup. It was raining, so we decided to go home through the mountains. Bone and I loved riding in the mountains in the rain. We put an old Stones tape in the tape deck, turned up the volume, and drove through the storm singing along to "Have Mercy." Halfway up this really steep road, the back of the truck opened up and everything slid out. We didn't hear the crash because we were singing so loudly. We didn't realize what had happened until Bone looked in the mirror and saw Leonardo's new home scattered all over the road behind us. You should have seen the two of us lugging it all back to the pickup. I nearly wet myself, I was laughing so much.

For the first time in ages I stopped wondering what Bill was doing without me and wondered what Bone and Hope were doing without me, instead. What music was Bone playing in the pickup? Were they singing along? Would they stop in our favourite diner, the Tex-Mex one with the great salsa, on the way back? All of a sudden I really missed them. Well, maybe not Hope so much. Hope hadn't really changed since I'd fallen in love, she was still my best friend even though I didn't see her very often, but things with Bone had changed. And I really wished that they hadn't. By the time Harry was running through the night to find Sally I was almost in tears.

Bill had had to take someone else's shift Saturday afternoon, which was why he never got around to calling me. It was their busiest day of the week, so he still had to work that night, but he had enough time to drop by with a video he wanted me to see.

I was pretty excited. I hardly ever got to see Bill alone, and since my mother was still out with John, it meant we had the whole house to ourselves.

Even though we'd been going out for over a week now, Bill had never really been in my house except to stand in the living-room, jangling his keys while he waited for me to get ready. He'd never seen my room; he'd never even seen Leonardo. So the first thing I did when Bill arrived was take him to meet my tortoise.

Bill followed me into my room. "Wow," he said, looking around with this kind of stunned expression on his face. "You sure have a lot of feathers."

I did have a lot of feathers – they were stuck all over the place – but I never really noticed them myself any more. "Bone and I kind of got into the habit of collecting them," I explained.

"Your room sure doesn't look like most girls' rooms," said Bill. He laughed. "Feathers, posters of lizards ... if I didn't know better, I might think you were a little weird."

I laughed. "Leonardo," I called, going straight for the vivarium. I carefully lifted the lid. A smell of rot drifted into the air. It must've been longer since I'd cleaned it than I'd thought. "Leonardo, I've brought someone to see you."

Bill came up beside me. "I thought you were kidding about having a turtle," he said.

"You did?" I was so surprised I didn't even point out that Leonardo was a tortoise, not a turtle. "But I told you all about him." Which I had. I'd told him how my mother found Leonardo on one of her jobs. The people who owned him thought he was dead but he wasn't, he was under the bathtub. And about the time Leonardo got out and Hope and I practically tore the whole house apart looking for him. I'd cried for two nights because I thought he was lost for good. And I told him how much Leonardo loved watercress. The minute he smelled it his little head went up and his little feet started moving as fast as they could go.

Bill shrugged. "I've never known a girl who liked turtles. I thought you were talking about a stuffed animal."

If anyone else had said he'd thought I was talking about a soft toy when I was talking about Leonardo, I'd have thought there was something radically wrong with him. What Bone called being a couple of cups short of a gallon. But with Bill it didn't sound stupid, it just sounded sweet. I could hear myself telling Hope about it: *Isn't Bill adorable, Hope? He thought Leonardo came from Mattell and not the Mediterranean.*

186

"You're too much." I giggled. I slipped my arm through his. "Well?" I asked. "Isn't he great?"

Leonardo gazed up, waiting to see which of us had the food. Bill gazed down. "I'm really more a dog man myself," he said. "I mean, turtles don't really do much, do they? Most of the time they just impersonate rocks."

That was when Leonardo bit him.

The video Bill had brought over was a thriller. I'd been hoping for something romantic – or even a little interesting. I tried not to show my disappointment.

"If you like *Psycho,* you're going to love this," Bill said as he pulled me down on the couch beside him.

About halfway through, Bill declared an intermission and I went into the kitchen to get us something to eat. I can't say I was disappointed to have to break off like that. I liked sitting close to Bill, burying my face in his shoulder at the bloodiest parts, but other than that I was obviously missing something. Except for a few good one-liners, it seemed like one of those "seen one, you've seen them all" kind of thrillers to me.

I was just pouring the chips into a bowl when the phone rang. I picked it up automatically.

"What happened to you?" asked Hope. "I

thought you were going to call me about coming over later."

"I was," I said immediately. "I am. I lost track of the time." I'd totally forgotten.

"So what about it?" asked Hope. "You want to hang out?"

Bill appeared in the doorway. "What happened?" he whispered. "Violence always affects my appetite. I'm starving."

I put my hand over the receiver. "It's Hope. I'll be off in a minute."

"Oh, guess what happened on the way back this afternoon," said Hope. "Bone and I stopped in that field on the back road to Santa Clara. You know, the one with all the gopher holes?" Her voice became excited. "And guess what, Mike. We found an arrowhead! Wait'll you see it. It's probably hundreds of years old."

I couldn't believe it. After all these years of searching, Bone finally found something, while I was watching some cop with an attitude take on a small army by himself. "Gee," I said. "That's great."

Hope got all involved in describing how and where they found the arrowhead.

But I was only half listening. I'd expected Bill to go back to the living-room, but instead he'd moved behind me and circled me with his arms. It was pretty difficult to concentrate on arrowheads with him pressed against me like that.

Bill started tickling my neck.

Hope thought they should give the arrowhead to the museum in Santa Clara, but Bone wanted to put it back in the ground where they'd found it.

"We agree that it doesn't belong to us," Hope rattled on. "You know, that it belongs to history, but I think it should be seen by people and Bone thinks it shouldn't. He thinks it should be allowed to stay in its proper resting place."

"Um," I said.

Bill started blowing in my ear.

"What do you think?" asked Hope. "Would you put it back?"

"Well…" I pulled away from Bill as gently as I could so I wouldn't hurt his feelings, but he didn't take the hint.

"Mike?" Hope shouted. "Mike? Are you still there?"

Bill's tongue went in my ear. I'd never had anybody's tongue in my ear before. It felt really weird.

"Sorry," I said, trying not to laugh. "Yeah, I'm still here."

"I mean I do understand what Bone means," Hope continued, "but every time I touch it I get a thrill just imagining what it was like around here then…"

I totally lost track of her words. Having a tongue in my ear was strange, but not unpleasant.

Hope came to the end of her imaginings. "So what do you think?"

Think? Who could think? The weirdness had passed and I was feeling a little thrilled myself.

"What?" I said.

Bill started nuzzling my hair.

"What's going on?" snapped Hope. "Is there someone with you, Mike? What are you doing?"

"Nothing," I said. "Just hold on a second, will you?" I put my hand over the mouthpiece again. "Bill..." I pleaded.

"You keep talking," he whispered. "Pretend I'm not here."

"I can't—" I began.

He put his lips on mine.

"Mike?" screamed Hope. "Mike, what is going on?"

"I'll call you back," I promised. "I can't talk now."

I was still holding the receiver when Hope hung up.

After Bill left, I flopped around in a state of cosmic meltdown from spending nearly three whole hours with him all by myself. It was weird, but in a way I kind of felt as though I'd been at this terrific party, where I was afraid of breaking something. You know, a party at

Steven Spielberg's house or something. Everything's perfect – the people, the decorations, the food, the music – and you're really happy to be there and enjoying yourself, but you can't stop worrying that you're going to drop one of Steve's crystal glasses or spill something on the rug. So even though you don't want the party to end, you're kind of relieved when it's over and you can go home and not be afraid you're going to say the wrong thing or leave a glass ring on the table.

The house felt kind of empty. I was used to spending time on my own. I could spend a whole weekend in my room, reading, or an entire afternoon sitting in the backyard, watching Leonardo wobbling around his outdoor run. But now I didn't know what to do with myself. I decided to take a bath. But then I got worried that Bill might call when he got to the restaurant, just to say hi. Because we only had the wall phone in the kitchen I couldn't bring it into the bathroom with me, so I put the answering machine on. Then I brought the portable cassette player from my room, lit some candles, and dumped the rest of my mother's bath oil into the tub. I lay there for hours, listening to Nirvana and watching the shadows from the candles flicker on the walls, thinking about Bill, trying to remember everything he'd said. I couldn't really remember much. The afternoon just kind of swirled around my mind like a cloud.

When I finally came out of the bathroom, there was a message on the machine. It wasn't Bill. It was my mother. I shouldn't wait to eat supper, they were going to be later than they'd planned.

I wasn't really hungry, but I made myself a sandwich. Then I sat on the couch for a while, staring at the ceiling, wondering what to do. I didn't feel like working on my paper, or reading a book, or even watching TV. All I could hear was the silence. All of a sudden I really felt like talking. "Yakking" Bill called it. "I don't know how girls can spend so much time on the phone," he'd said. "Yak, yak, yak." That was when I remembered Hope. I'd promised to call her back. I checked the time. It was still early enough for me to go over to her house – or for her to come over to mine.

Hope's mother answered the phone. I could hear Mr Perez shouting in the background.

"Hope's not here, Mike," said Mrs Perez. "She went out."

"Out?" How could she could go out when she knew I was going to call to come over?

"Well, it *is* Saturday night," said Hope's mother.

Going to the movies on Sunday night was Bill's idea. "The guys and I usually play basketball Sunday nights," he'd said when he called that morning, "but after a double shift yesterday I'm going to be too tired. Why don't we go to a movie?"

It was my idea to ask Hope and Bone to go with us. It came to me when I was talking to Hope later that morning. I guess I was feeling a little guilty about Saturday. Anyway, when I called her, Hope said she felt like we never did anything together any more so I suggested the movies. I didn't think Bill would mind. I had this image of the four of us hanging out together; of all of us being friends. Hope said yes right away. "I was wondering if I was ever going to meet Bill," she said. Bone said he already knew Bill Copeland as well as he wanted to, but when I told him Hope was coming he changed his mind. He said he couldn't let Hope go through a night with Bill without his moral support.

Bill thought I was joking when I told him.

"You're kidding me, right?" asked Bill.

"Well, no," I stammered. "I – I didn't think you'd mind."

Bill sighed. "I don't mind going out with Hope," said Bill. "She sounds all right. But Bobby—" He gave me a look. "I know he's your childhood friend and everything," Bill went on, "but he just better not talk about music all night."

The evening went downhill from there.

We'd arranged to meet outside the new

movie complex in Santa Clara at six o'clock. Bill and I were there at six. Hope and Bone weren't. After about ten minutes, Bill began to fidget. He hated waiting. He hated going into the theatre after the lights had gone out. He didn't like to miss the beginning of the programme.

"Maybe we should go ahead and get our tickets," Bill suggested. He glanced behind us at the steady line of people going through the main door. "In case they sell out."

"We can't buy our tickets," I reminded him. "We haven't decided what we're going to see yet."

"I know what I want to see," said Bill.

I started to laugh, but at that moment Hope and Bone appeared at the end of the street. Bill groaned. "Jeez, look at Bobby, will you? He looks like a mechanic."

It was true, Bone could have passed for a mechanic. His hands, most of his face, and a lot of his shirt were filthy with grease. But there was something almost critical in the way Bill said "mechanic".

I slipped my arm through his. "There's nothing wrong with mechanics," I said lightly.

"I didn't say there was," answered Bill. "But that doesn't mean I want to spend my free time with one."

I was about to point out that he didn't seem to mind spending his free time with the daughter of a plumber, but Hope came rushing up to us just then.

"We're sorry we're late," she apologized breathlessly. "We had a flat."

"It doesn't matter," I said quickly, ignoring the fact that neither Bill nor Bone were saying anything. "You're here now. Let's decide what we're seeing and get our tickets."

Of the six movies playing, two were for kids, two were thrillers, one was a love story and the other was the comedy Hope and I had planned to see the week before.

Nobody wanted to see the kids' shows or the love story. Bone and Hope wanted to see the comedy by the Chinese director. Bill wanted to see one of the thrillers. I didn't know what I wanted to see. If I went along with Hope and Bone, Bill would think I was ganging up on him with my friends. But if I picked the thriller, Bone and Hope would think I was just saying that because of Bill.

"I don't like foreign movies," said Bill. He smiled at Hope and Bone. "They're usually so depressing."

I could see that Hope was going to explain that it was a comedy and it wasn't really foreign, the director just happened to be Chinese, but Bone spoke first.

"And the rest of us don't like thrillers," said Bone.

"Michelle does," said Bill. He slipped an

arm around my shoulder. "Don't you, Michelle?"

I couldn't look at Hope and Bone, not the way they were looking at me. Like they believed I'd really told Bill that I liked thrillers. Like they were waiting for me to tell him that I didn't. I looked at Bill. He was smiling at me confidently. I opened my mouth. Nothing came out.

Bill squeezed my shoulder affectionately. "Stop kidding around, Michelle. You said you liked the video we watched yesterday."

This time when I opened my mouth something did come out. "Well – I – uh—"

"You see?" said Bill. He grinned at Bone and Hope. "That means it's two against two."

"What do you suggest we do about that?" asked Bone. "Have a duel?"

Bill led the way through the gloom. Hope and I always sat dead in the middle, but Bill liked to sit on the left-hand side, right on the aisle. "Now remember," he said, talking softly into my ear. "You just bury your face in my shoulder if it gets too violent for you, and I'll tell you when you can look."

Suddenly I remembered what the advantage of seeing a thriller with Bill was. I could sit in his lap if I wanted to and everyone would figure it was just because I was frightened. "Thanks," I whispered back.

"The pleasure is all mine," Bill said, grinning.

I probably would have enjoyed a duel a lot more than I enjoyed the thriller. Not that I paid that much attention to it. I sat through most of it with my head against Bill's chest, listening to his heart beat while my own melted with contentment. When everybody else screamed, I screamed, too. Then Bill would hold me tighter. "Close your eyes," he'd whisper, and I'd close my eyes. I'd never felt happier. I was so happy that I stopped feeling bad about Bone and Hope.

Bone and Hope had gone to the comedy.

Afterwards, the four of us went out for a snack. Bill suggested that Hope and Bone pick the place. "That way I know I won't run into any of my friends," he joked to me.

Hope picked the Tex-Mex diner.

It was in a long, narrow brick building. There were booths on either side of the one large room and mismatched tables in the middle. There were chilli pepper Christmas tree lights strung across the ceiling and odd pieces of junk-store treasures all over the walls. My favourite thing in the diner, aside from the food, was a chrome-and-neon moon clock, but Hope liked the ancient Victrola, and Bone liked the ragged bison head best. We sat in a corner booth.

Bill squinted at the stained sheet of cardboard the waiter had put in front of him. "I believe in atmosphere," he said, "but it's so dark you can hardly read the menu."

"It doesn't matter," said Bone. "Everything's good."

Bill didn't pay any attention. He was looking around as though he were thinking of buying the place. "And look at all this junk. It's like a warehouse in here."

Hope gave me a look.

I gave Bill an affectionate nudge. "It has its own eccentric charm," I said. "That's why we love it."

Bill laughed. "Oh, come on, Michelle. Look at the way this place is decorated..." He nodded toward the bison head. "It's not even hygienic."

"I like the way it's decorated," said Hope a little defensively.

"Wait'll you taste the salsa," I told Bill. "It's the best in the world."

Bill didn't really care about the salsa. He started explaining how decor and atmosphere are just as important to the success of a restaurant as the quality of the food – maybe even more important.

Bone started talking about the movie he and Hope had seen.

"A restaurant has to be co-ordinated," said Bill. "This place is such a mishmash it doesn't have any atmosphere."

"I think the funniest part was the fight at breakfast," said Bone.

Hope stopped looking at Bill. "Oh, wasn't that hilarious?" She gave Bone a poke. "Tell them about it," she urged him. She looked at me. "You would have lost it," she said.

Bone began describing the fight at breakfast at about the same second that Bill began telling me what else was wrong with the diner.

I didn't know which of them to look at or listen to. No matter what I did, someone was going to be mad at me. And Hope was no help. She was giving all her attention to Bone. You'd think she hadn't watched the movie with him. I decided to follow Leonardo's example. When he felt confused or threatened, he went into his shell. I went to the toilet.

Hope had a special meeting of the orchestra early on Monday morning, which meant that I didn't see her to talk about Sunday night until lunch. Fortunately, Bone couldn't eat with us because he had something else to do. I didn't feel like rehashing the evening with Bone. I knew I hadn't heard the last about liking thrillers.

"So?" I said as soon as we sat down. "What did you think?"

Hope opened her lunch box. "About what?"

I groaned. "Oh, come on, Hope. You know about what. About Bill. What did you think? Isn't he great?"

Hope unwrapped her sandwich. "He's OK," she said, her eyes on her lunch. "He seems really nice."

"OK?" I shrieked. "Nice?" I'd expected a little more enthusiasm from my best friend. I knew Hope well enough to know that she probably thought it was a little weird of Bill not to go along with the rest of us on the movie, but aside from that he'd been his usual wonderful self. She had to like him more than "OK". "Stop kidding around," I ordered. "Admit that Bill's the most fantastic boy on the planet."

Hope finally looked at me. She smiled. "Well, he certainly knows more about decorating restaurants than most of them."

I didn't smile back. "What's that supposed to mean?" I demanded.

Hope shrugged. "Nothing. Just that he knows a lot about decorating restaurants."

I pushed my lunch away. "I thought you said you liked Bill," I said accusingly.

Hope put down her sandwich. "I do like him," she said quietly. "He's OK. But if you want me to be totally honest, Mike..." Her voice trailed off.

Whenever somebody says she's going to be totally honest it usually means she's going to tell you something you don't want to hear. I didn't care. I knew Bill, and Hope didn't. Anything she said was just her opinion. "If I want you to be totally honest, what?"

Hope frowned at the table for a second, then she took a deep breath. "If you want me to be totally honest, I really don't see what the big deal is. I mean, he's nice enough and he's cute and everything, but..."

"But what?"

Hope raised her head and looked me in the eye. "But he really doesn't seem ... well ... right for you."

It's just as well I'd pushed my lunch away. I would have choked to death if I'd been eating when she said that.

"Not right for me? What are you talking about not right for me?"

"He's not from the same batch," said Hope flatly.

I made a face. "Now you sound like Bone."

"And you sound like Bill lately," said Hope.

"I do not."

"You do," Hope insisted. "'Bill says ... Bill thinks ... Bill told me ...' What are you all of a sudden, a human commercial for Bill Copeland?"

"I'm in love," I said patiently. "That's the way people act when they're in love. Remember?"

Hope shook her head. "It's more than that, Mike. You've changed since you started going out with Bill."

I leaned back in my chair. "Really?" I folded my arms in front of me. "How?"

"You're going to basketball games and watching thrillers, for a start—"

I had to laugh. "And you've started playing Cajun music," I countered. "Why is it all right for you to do something you never did before, but not for me?"

"That's not the same kind of thing and you know it," said Hope. "Can't you see what you're doing, Mike? You're bending over backward to like the things that Bill likes, but really you two don't have very much in common."

My laughter became more shrill. "Oh, please ... Bill and I have megatons in common."

"Name one thing besides the fact that you're both human and live in California." She sneered.

"I've told you already." I sneered back. "The dentist, the scars, Cel-Ray soda..."

"Something important," said Hope.

I figured it was the shock of being attacked like this by my best friend, but I couldn't think of anything that Hope would consider important. So I decided to launch an attack of my own.

"This is all Bone, isn't it?" I demanded. "Just because he doesn't like Bill, he put these ideas in your head."

Hope shook her head in disbelief. "You don't get it, do you?"

"Get what?"

"Why Bone was so upset when you fell for Bill."

What was there not to get? "Because he never liked him," I answered immediately. "Bone thinks if he doesn't like someone, no one else should like him either."

"No, it wasn't," said Hope. Her voice was quiet again. "It was because Bone liked you."

"Well, of course he likes me." I was still laughing. "He's my—"

"No," said Hope. She was shaking her head again. "I mean *liked* you."

I stopped laughing. "Bone? Bone liked *me*?"

"Only he didn't want to risk losing your friendship if you didn't feel the same way." She made a face. "He didn't think you did."

I hadn't. I'd always thought Bone would never be interested in me. We were too close friends. And I'd been right. I had to be. Hope must be making this up.

"How do you know all this?" I demanded.

Hope looked back at me, her expression blank. "Bone told me."

I just sat there for a second, trying to take it in. I couldn't. "Oh, please… Bone wouldn't tell you something like that. He's too private. He—"

"—had to tell me," finished Hope. "He wanted me to know before he asked me out."

I smiled, but not from happiness, from confusion. "Bone asked you out?"

Hope leaned towards me across the table. "I didn't want you to find out like this, Mike," she said gently. "I really didn't. Both of us were going to talk to you—"

"Oh, really?" Suddenly I was really upset. How could they? How could my two best friends start going out together and not tell me? I introduced them. When were they going to let me know what was happening? When Bone reminded me that I'd promised I'd be best man at his wedding if he ever did get married? "I don't believe this!" I was shrieking slightly. "When did this happen? How?"

"I don't really know." Hope shrugged. "We started hanging out when you got so interested in Bill, you know, we both missed you, and then ... well, I guess we just got to know each other better." She smiled shyly. "One thing kind of led to another."

"And all the while there wasn't one minute when either of you could tell me what was going on?" I was shrieking in earnest now.

"We were waiting for the right moment," said Hope, calmly. "Only it never came."

"How were you going to know it when it came?" I asked. "Was it going to be wearing a sign or something?"

"It would have had to be wearing a sign to get your attention," said Hope.

I couldn't wait to tell my mother what had happened. I knew she'd be as shocked and outraged as I was. "Can you believe it?" I'd say. "I'm their best friend and they didn't even give me a hint!"

My mother must have had a pretty unbusy day, because she was already home when I got back. She was in the kitchen, working out her schedule. John was stirring something on the stove. He was wearing a checked apron over his T-shirt and jeans. He must have had an unbusy day, too.

I collapsed on the chair across from my mother and wrapped my arms around myself.

She raised her eyes. "What's with you?" She lowered her eyes. "You look upset."

"I am upset."

My mother kept writing. "What's wrong? Did you have a fight with Hope?"

"Kind of."

John looked over. "I've got just the thing to cheer you up," he informed me. "We're having Lasagne Sugarman tonight." Sugarman was John's last name.

"Don't forget, honey, there's more olive oil in the cabinet," said my mother.

For a second I thought she was talking to me. "What?" I asked.

John said, "Gotcha."

I looked from my mother to John and then back to my mother. Something wasn't normal, but I was too worked up about Hope and Bone to think about it.

"So," said my mother. "What was the fight about?"

John was peering into the pot on the stove. "You want to see if you think this needs more oregano?"

My mother got up and went over to the stove. She opened her mouth for the spoonful of sauce John was lifting toward her. "Perfect," she pronounced.

"You're not going to believe this," I said to their backs, "but Hope is going out with Bone!" My voice rose in indignation. "And they never told me!"

They turned around at the same time.

"Well?" I demanded. "Don't you think that's unbelievable?"

It was John who answered. "You mean you didn't know?"

"No, I didn't know. How could I know when nobody bothered to tell me?" I stared at them and they stared back at me. And then, as Bone would have said, a light went on. "You knew?" I shrieked. "Are you saying that you *knew*?"

John glanced at my mother. "I just assumed when they came over together the other day …"

"It was kind of obvious," said my mother.

"It wasn't obvious to me," I snapped back.

My mother and John started to laugh at the same instant.

I was appalled. Really appalled. Here I'd expected my mother to be sympathetic and supportive and instead she was standing there, clutching our mechanic while the two of them choked with laughter.

"I'm glad you two think it's so funny!" I shouted. "Because I don't. I don't think it's funny at all."

My mother recovered first. "We're not laughing at *you*, Mike," she said. "It's just that ... well ... you haven't exactly been paying much attention to anyone else lately."

She was trying to make me feel guilty. And she was succeeding. I could feel my lower lip tremble. "Why is everybody on my case all of a sudden?"

My mother looked at John. John looked at my mother. "You want me to take a walk?" he asked her.

"No." She shook her head. "You're part of this, too."

I looked from one to the other. I had no idea what they were talking about. "Part of what?" I asked.

My mother came over and put an arm around me. "Part of what you haven't been paying attention to," she said.

I was definitely having one of those days.

I'd been right in thinking that things weren't normal between my mother and John. It turned out that John was cooking supper for us because they'd been trying to get me to go out to dinner with them so they could talk to me, but I'd always refused to go. What they wanted to talk to me about was *them*.

I tried to take this in. "What?"

My mother blushed. "You know..." She smiled. "Now that John and I are seeing each other—"

"What?"

"You know." John laughed. "Seeing each other, dating seriously, going steady..."

"What?" I couldn't seem to say anything else.

My mother gave me one of her really concerned looks. "Are you saying you didn't even suspect that John and I were going out together, either?"

I shook my head. "How could I? You didn't tell me any more than Hope did."

My mother had this way of just looking at you that was the equivalent of having a stadium full of people jumping up and down shouting, "Have you lost your mind?" That was the way she was looking at me now.

"Oh, yes, I did," she said. She'd told me right from the start, it seemed. The day after she and John went to the wedding together.

She'd told me what a great time they'd had, how they'd talked and joked till the bride and groom left for their honeymoon, and then had gone to an all-night diner, where they'd sat talking and joking some more until two in the morning. My mother accused me of being self-obsessed. She wanted to know what I'd thought about the fact that she and John had been spending so much time together if it hadn't dawned on me that they were seeing each other.

"I just thought you were hanging out together more than usual," I mumbled. "You know, because you're friends."

"We are friends," said John. He smiled at my mother. "It just took us a while to figure out how good."

"Maybe like Bone and Hope," said my mother.

I was tempted to call Hope as soon as supper was over to tell her about my mother and John, but when I thought about it I didn't really feel like talking to Hope. Besides, Hope would probably be on the phone with Bone, telling him what she'd said to me. I called Bill.

Just the sound of his voice made me feel better. Knowing I had Bill made everything all right.

"I'm so glad you're home," I said in a rush. "Wait'll you hear what's happened." I told him about Hope and Bone.

"So what?" asked Bill. "I mean, I agree they should have told you, but it's not that big a deal." He laughed. "Maybe Hope was embarrassed…"

Embarrassed was one reason that hadn't occurred to me. "Embarrassed? Embarrassed about what?"

He laughed again. "You know, Michelle. About going out with Bone. I mean, she must be a little desperate. Dating Bone's like wearing jeans to the senior prom."

Wearing jeans to the senior prom didn't sound like that bad an idea to me. It was better than looking like a Barbie doll. At least you'd be able to dance without tripping over your heels. But I didn't want to get sidetracked into another conversation. "You mean it's inappropriate?"

"That's a nice way of putting it," said Bill.

I decided not to get sidetracked into that conversation either. "That's not all, though," I went on. "When I got home, my mother and John were in the kitchen—"

Bill cut me off. "Look, I'm sorry, Michelle, but I was on my way out when you called. Why don't I phone you when I get back?"

I said that was fine. I told him I'd wait up for his call.

My mother and John wanted me to play Scrabble with them. Bone, Hope and I loved

Scrabble. Only we always played by our own rules. Renegade Scrabble we called it. You were allowed to make up words as long as they made some kind of sense. "Conversate" for talk. "Dedigest" for vomit. "Slurf" to describe the way Leonardo fooled around in his water. "Snarfle" to describe the way Bone ate. I didn't feel like Scrabble that night. I was exhausted and numb from the shocks of the day. I went to my room to wait for Bill to call back. *Hope and Bone. Bone and Hope.* Their names repeated themselves in my head like a chant. *Bone and Hope.* I finished my homework, uninterrupted by the sound of a ringing telephone. *Hope and Bone.* I straightened out my desk. *Bone and Hope.* I lined my shoes up under my bed. *Hope and Bone.* I went to the window and pulled the curtains aside. There were only a few really low-wattage stars in the sky.

I felt a little guilty about it, but I couldn't help wondering what would have happened if Bone and I had gotten together. I decided that not much would have happened. Everything else would have gone on just as it was, only more so. Bone and I would be just as we'd always been, but with kissing. I gazed out at the feebly flickering stars. What would it be like to kiss Bone? I closed the curtains again. If I wanted to know that, I'd have to ask Hope.

The phone next door began to ring. I threw

myself on my bed and stared at the ceiling. *Hope and Bone. Bone and Hope.* Chants were supposed to help make things clearer, but that one didn't. It just made me feel even more confused. I didn't have any trouble accepting the fact of my mom and John. Now that I knew, even I couldn't understand why I hadn't figured it out before. It was pretty obvious. But Hope and Bone were different. I'd always been Bone's favourite person and now Hope was. Even though I knew it was childish, it upset me. I felt kind of betrayed. I figured that must have been how Bone felt when I fell in love with Bill, and it made me feel a little bit better.

Bone and Hope … Hope and Bone … I hoped Bill wouldn't stay out too long.

I fell asleep with my clothes on. I dreamed of Bill.

LOVE HURTS

Bone must have been feeling guilty, because he tried to talk to me about him and Hope after English on Tuesday.

"Hope said she told you about us yesterday," said Bone. He picked up his books from his desk. "You know, I'm sorry, Mike. I really wanted us to tell you together."

I picked up my books and headed for the door before he could add, "But you never gave me a chance."

"It's OK," I said. "It would have been nice not to be the last to know, but I understand."

Bone trotted behind me. "Well, I was thinking, Mike... maybe you could come over this afternoon and we could talk about it."

"There's nothing to talk about," I assured him. "Really."

Bone shrugged. "OK, so why don't you come over and we won't talk about it."

I gave him one of my brightest smiles. "I can't," I said. "It's Tuesday. Bill's playing basketball this afternoon."

For once he didn't crack a basketball joke. "Well, maybe tomorrow, then," said Bone.

I said, "Yeah, maybe tomorrow." Even though I knew this was going to be one of those times when tomorrow didn't come.

I really didn't feel like hanging out with either Bone or Hope at the moment, even though in a weird way I really missed them.

It wasn't that I was mad, or even that I was feeling hurt. What I felt now was awkward. Bone and I still sat next to each other in English, and the three of us still had lunch together, and Hope and I still walked to and from school together, but it wasn't the same. They acted just as they always had, but I didn't know how to act around them any more. I felt like a third wheel. A third wheel on a mountain bike, this little bitsy wheel that kind of wobbled alongside the other two. The first two wheels needed each other now, but neither of them needed the third one. I decided just to stay away from them for a while, until things seemed normal to me, too. Stay away from them and concentrate on Bill.

Mr Hunter was talking about fairy tales. "Fairy tales," said Mr Hunter, "are a fantastic way of expressing our real fears and emotions. They help us learn to deal with life. Unlike realistic stories, which are concerned with our external reality, fairy tales are concerned with our inner reality." Mr Hunter started to drone on about how fairy tales were still very much a part of our lives. And I started thinking about my inner reality.

At the moment my inner reality was a little bleak.

It was already Wednesday and I hadn't talked to Bill since Monday night. I'd waited all afternoon for him to pick me up for the game, but he never came. I called his house and left a message on the machine: "Hi, Bill. It's Mike. Please phone me when you get home." Maybe he never got home that night, or maybe he didn't get my message, but he never called.

Mr Hunter scribbled the names of some fairy tales on the board and I wrote B. C. in the margin of my notebook and drew a heart around it. The heart was cracked in the middle. I drew a dark cloud around it.

I got so involved in thinking about Bill that I totally forgot where I was, until a shadow fell over my notebook. I looked up. Mr Hunter was standing in front of me, giving me an unpleasant smile. "Am I boring you more than usual, Miss Brindisi?" he asked. "Is that why whenever I look over at you you're staring into space with your mouth open like a fish out of water?"

I kept my eyes on Mr Hunter, but I could feel the rest of the class smiling. "I... no... I... That's not true," I stammered. "I've been listen—"

"Have you?" Mr Hunter lifted my loose-leaf binder from my desk. "And are these your notes?" He held the book so the rest of the class could see it. "I don't remember saying anything like 'Bill + Me = 4ever'." He cleared his throat. "This isn't a maths class, Miss Brindisi," he boomed. "It's English."

The bell rang just as everyone started to laugh.

"So," said Bone as we left English together, "have a good time yesterday?"

I glanced at him to see if he was being sarcastic, but he was looking back at me with genuine interest. I was almost tempted to tell him the truth, that I'd sat in my room, watching the digital clock and thinking about him and Hope all afternoon. But the last thing I needed was for Bone to feel sorry for me.

"Yeah," I lied. "It was terrific. Bill scored three baskets."

"So," said Bone. "You on for this afternoon?"

Having started lying, I decided to continue. "I'm really sorry," I said, sounding sorry, "but I promised Bill I'd help him run some errands for the restaurant after school."

I expected Bone to make some crack, like "By God! He's already got her working for him," but he didn't. "No sweat," said Bone. "Tomorrow is another day."

Bill didn't call me Wednesday, either. I sat home all afternoon, thinking of reasons why he hadn't called. He'd lost my number. But if he had, why didn't he come over and ask for it? He must have realized I spent most of my time waiting for him to show up. He couldn't think I was always home when he called because I had nothing else to do. I answered that one right away. He hadn't come over because he'd been too busy with work and college and playing basketball with his friends.

Too busy just to drop by for five minutes? It occurred to me that while I'd drop anything to be with Bill, Bill wouldn't drop anything to be with me. I shoved the thought out of my mind.

Maybe he was sick. He ate at Chez Moi a lot. Food poisoning wasn't out of the question. My mother got food poisoning the first time she went out with my dad. It lasted five days. She thought he was trying to kill her. Or if it wasn't food poisoning, Bill might have the flu. Or he might have been injured. Anything could have happened: an accident in the restaurant, a broken bone playing ball, a car crash...

The thought that Bill might be lying in a

coma in the hospital, or something even worse, convinced me. I didn't want him to think that I didn't care enough about him to be concerned when I didn't hear from him. I couldn't wait for him to call me. If he were in a coma, I could be waiting a long time. I had to call him.

His mother answered the phone. Bill wasn't home.

I wasn't as relieved as I'd thought I'd be to find out he was still alive. Now I still didn't know why he hadn't called.

"And who is this?" asked Mrs Copeland.

"It's Michelle."

"Michelle who?" That threw me for a second. How many Michelles did Bill know?

"Brindisi," I finally answered. "Michelle Brindisi."

But this didn't have the effect I'd expected, either. Mrs Copeland didn't say, "Oh, Michelle *Brindisi*!" as though she'd heard a lot about me – as though she knew I was Bill's new girlfriend. She didn't say anything.

"Well…" I said lamely. "Maybe you could tell him Michelle called." I was tempted to give her my number, just in case, but I didn't. I was kind of hurt that he hadn't told his mother about us. Bill showed a lot of initiative when it came to dealing with the restaurant. He could show a little when it came to dealing with me.

On Thursday it was Hope who asked me if I'd had fun with Bill the day before. I said yes. I didn't need Hope feeling sorry for me either. Hope wanted me to hang out with her after school, but even though I knew Bill had a late class, I said I was doing something with him. "I guess there's no chance of video night tomorrow," said Hope. I said that there wasn't. Even if it turned out that I didn't have a date, watching movies all night with Hope and Bone when we were all just friends was one thing. Watching them with a couple was something else.

I spent most of Thursday evening feeling sorry for myself. I was beginning to feel that if a relationship was a boat, I was in this one all by myself. Unless his friends were around and he got a little distracted, Bill was great when we were together. But when we weren't together I wondered if he ever really thought of me at all. *But he said you were different*, I reminded myself. *He said you looked good together*. I thought of Hal and Layla. When Bill was with them he was a lot like Hal. *Bill's been changing his image*, I'd heard Layla say. I couldn't help wondering if I was just part of that change.

"You're not coming out?" my mother shouted from the hall. "What do you mean, you're not coming out?"

Bill hadn't called on Friday, either. I had nothing to come out for.

"I mean I'm staying in here," I shouted back. Beside me, the radio was playing, only something strange had happened to Bill's favourite station. Most of the songs they used to play when I first started listening had been about falling in love and being so happy. But that Saturday morning most of them were about falling in love and wishing you were dead. Which was pretty much how I was feeling.

My mother wasn't going to give up so easily. "Are you sure you're not coming down with something?" she persisted.

"Terminal love," I felt like shouting back. *"I've come down with a case of terminal love."* "I'm all right," I said instead. "Really. I just don't feel like coming out right now."

"It's a beautiful day," my mother went on. "You can't spend it in your room. It's not natural."

Which just showed how much she knew about love. All the singers of the sad love songs knew that now that their hearts were broken there was nothing left for them. If they never came out of their rooms it wouldn't matter, they would never be happy again. Which was pretty much how I was feeling, too. Maybe Bill had no intention of ever calling me again. Maybe he was out with his friends and had

220

forgotten all about me. Maybe he was giving some other girl a ride home from the mall.

"I'll come out later," I screamed back. "Just leave me alone for a while."

"What about Leonardo?" countered my mother. "You haven't cleaned him since last week. And it doesn't look as though you've fed him for a while."

"He's all right, too," I assured her. "I'll do it later."

"Later when?" asked my mother.

"Later on."

"You'll do it now," said my mother, "or I'll take the door off the hinges and come in after you."

Since it was such a beautiful day, I put Leonardo in his run in the backyard and sat on the patio to work on my English paper. My mother came out to do her annual bout of gardening, which meant she was watering the herbs.

"Are you sure Leonardo's all right?" she shouted to me. "He doesn't look right."

I looked up. She was kneeling in the grass, holding a few mint leaves over the side of the run. "He's fine," I assured her. "It's just taking him a little longer than usual to come out of hibernation."

"Come on, Leonardo," coaxed my mother. "It's your favourite."

"Just drop it near him," I said. "He's playing

hard to get."

My mother leaned into the run. It almost looked as though she were going to kiss Leonardo's shell. "He stinks!" she shrieked.

"He's a tortoise," I answered. "That's how they smell."

"You mean that's how they smell if you forget to clean them," said my mother.

I turned back to my homework. It wasn't bad enough that she'd made me feel guilty about Hope and Bone, now she was making me feel guilty about Leonardo, too.

In the late morning my mother went into town; I stayed home but found it hard to concentrate on my paper.

I kept staring at the last line I'd written, which was pretty much the first as well. *When Sally and Harry met they disliked each other, then they became friends, then they fell in love.* Hope and Bone walked into my mind. His arm was around her. They were so close that Bone might have been an old coat Hope had over her shoulders. They were laughing. Bill and I walked into my mind. We were holding hands. We were laughing, too.

I leaned back over my chair to make sure the phone wasn't ringing inside. Silence. But maybe it had been ringing. I decided to check the machine again.

The tiny red light was as still as a stone. I

stood there looking at it for a few minutes. Should I call Bill? After all, it was nearly eleven. Even if he slept in because it was Saturday he was bound to be up by now...

"I'm afraid Bill's not here," Mrs Copeland informed me. "He went out early with Hal."

I said, "Oh."

"I believe they've gone sailing," said Mrs Copeland. "He's been working very hard all week, and it's such a beautiful day."

Even though I at least knew why he hadn't had a chance to call, the day didn't seem as beautiful as it had a few minutes ago.

"Oh," I mumbled. "Right. Sailing." I cleared my throat. "Did he say when he'd be back?"

"No." It almost sounded as though she'd sighed. "I'll tell him you called." She hung up the phone.

To tell the truth, I was pretty hurt that Bill had gone sailing with Hal. I figured they'd gone to the cove for the barbecue Layla had mentioned. A whole day out. Without me. As I thought about it I realized I was more than hurt. If you want the whole truth, I was mad. Even if it had been a last-minute thing, he could have asked me to go. He must have known that I'd drop anything else I was doing to be with him.

By six o'clock I figured that Bill's mother had probably forgotten to tell him I called, so

I called again.

Bill wasn't home yet. His mother thought he was probably playing basketball now. "Is this Michelle?" she wanted to know.

"Yes," I said. "Yes, it is."

This time she definitely sighed. "I did give him your message."

"Oh, I'm sure you did," I said quickly.

"Don't worry, Michelle," Mrs Copeland said flatly. "I'll tell him you called again."

My mother went over to John's Saturday night. She hesitated at the door. "Maybe I should have him come over here," she said. "We could get pizza or something." Even though the idea of having pizza with my mom and John was pretty appealing, I told her not to be ridiculous.

I smiled. "You go on." I said, "I've got to finish my paper anyway." I didn't need her to feel sorry for me, either.

My mother was pretending not to be studying me but I could tell from the way her lips were set that she was. The van keys jangled in her hand. "You're sure?"

"Yeah," I said. "Of course I'm sure." Since I'd fallen in love I was getting used to being by myself.

After she left I went into the kitchen to see if I finally felt like eating.

I opened the refrigerator door and stared in.

Apple juice ... orange juice ... lemonade ... pasta salad ... cheese ... tomatoes ... lettuce ... eggs ... my stomach growled. I decided to make myself a sandwich before I sat down to work.

There was a little lettuce and tomato left over, so after I finished eating I took it into my room to give to Leonardo. Leonardo wasn't there. I stood there staring at his empty vivarium for a few seconds, waiting for him to suddenly reappear from behind a rock or a plant. And then I remembered. Leonardo was in the backyard. I'd forgotten to bring him in.

I was a little worried that the neighbour's dog might have carried him off, but Leonardo was right where my mother had left him, in the near corner of his run.

"Come on, Leonardo..." I leaned over him in the dark. He was still in his shell. "Let's go inside. I've got some lettuce and tomato for you. You can even have a little cheese." He wasn't supposed to eat it, but Leonardo loved cheese.

As soon as I touched him I knew something was wrong.

I just stood there in the light from our neighbours' back porch, looking down at the dark shape of Leonardo Brindisi in the shadows. I'd killed my tortoise. Through neglect. Through my obsession with being in love.

"Oh, Leonardo..." I whispered. More or

less blind with tears, I bent down and gently lifted him from the cold, cold ground.

I didn't even think about what to do. With Leonardo in my arms, I ran into the house and dialled Hope's number.

"Oh, no," Hope wailed. "Are you sure?"

I stroked the black-and-yellow shell. "Yes." I sobbed. "No. I don't know. Oh, Hope, he doesn't even flinch when you poke him."

Someone started shouting behind her. "What's wrong? Is that Mike?" It was Bone.

"It's Leonardo," Hope told him. "Mike thinks he's dead."

Bone got on the phone. He didn't say hello or anything like that. He said, "What happened?"

I told him what had happened. I told him that Leonardo had been eating badly and that he'd begun to smell. I told him about leaving Leonardo outside all evening. I told him about finding Leonardo at the edge of the run, just plunked there like a stone. The more I told Bone, the more I cried. "It's my fault," I gabbled. "I didn't pay any attention to the uneaten food or the smell. I neglected him. I—"

"Don't be so hard on yourself," said Bone. "For all you know it was old age. Why don't you make yourself a cup of tea or something? We'll be right over."

I sat on the front stoop to wait for them. The

night was dark and restless. I'd never felt so alone in my life. I felt like a Komodo dragon on a chicken farm. All I could do was cry. It seemed like hours before Bone's pickup landed in the driveway, horn squawking and brakes squealing. Bone reached me first. He took Leonardo from my hands very gently. Hope came running up and threw her arms around me. "It's all right," she said. "We're here now." And it was kind of true. Things weren't all right, but they were better. I wasn't alone. There were a couple of other dragons on the farm.

"I'm sure I saw him blink," said Bone. He'd put Leonardo on the table, under the hanging lamp, and his own head flat on the table beside him, peering in. He turned his head away for a second. "Whew," whistled Bone. "If he isn't sick he's got a really bad case of halitosis."

"Maybe we should call the vet or the A.S.P.C.A.," Hope suggested.

"The vet won't be open now," I snuffled.

"He'll have an emergency number," said Hope.

Bone said, "Come on, Leonardo, blink again."

Hope said, "Have you tried offering him some cheese?"

I phoned Dr Abrams's emergency number while Hope tried cheese. The recorded voice said he'd call me back immediately.

"I just wish there was something we could do." I wiped a few more tears from my eyes. "What if he isn't dead yet, but he dies while we're waiting for the vet?"

"He isn't dead," said Bone. "I know he isn't. I think he's just depressed." He tilted his head and peered in again. "There must be some way of getting his attention."

Hope put down the piece of cheese she'd been holding. "Well, that didn't work."

Bone looked over at me. "What about music?" He gave me a smile. "You do own something other than Nirvana, don't you?"

"Bobby," said Hope.

"Just joking," said Bone.

I swallowed a sob. "Well, he always liked B.B. King." Whenever I played B.B. King, Leonardo would lift up his head as though he was listening. Once Bone even got him to sway a little.

"But he never liked Springsteen," said Hope. "He really hated 'Born to Run'."

Bone straightened up, snapping his fingers. "I know just the thing," he said, and he picked up Leonardo and ran out of the room. Hope and I followed. By the time we got to the living-room, Bone was already rummaging through the videos, Leonardo on his lap.

Hope and I sat beside them, telling our favourite Leonardo stories. The time Leonardo got lost in the house and Bone found him in the coat closet with his head through the hole he'd eaten in my mother's Panama hat. The time Leonardo got into the next-door neighbours' garden and ravaged their entire lettuce crop. The Halloween I dressed up as a hare and we took Leonardo trick-or-treating with us.

By the time Bone shouted "I've got it!" all three of us had tears in our eyes, but from laughing so much.

My mother and John walked through the door just as the first strains of the *Cheers* theme song came on.

"What's going on?" asked my mom. "You guys having a party?"

Leonardo stuck his nose out of his shell.

"No, but we will tomorrow," said Bone.

When the vet called back he said it sounded to him like depression. "You never can tell with tortoises," he told me. "They're more sensitive than you'd think." The vet said Leonardo was probably just in need of some attention. He said to call him right away if Leonardo seemed to get worse, but otherwise I could wait till Monday to bring him in for a check-up. Bone said he'd take us over in the truck after school.

Later, when he and Hope were leaving, the three of us stood on the porch saying goodbye. I thanked them again for coming and saving Leonardo's life.

"You don't have to thank us, Mike," said Hope. "We're friends, remember?"

"Yeah." I shook my head. "I remember." I took a deep breath. There was something I had to say, and it had to be then. "I just want you both to know that I'm really sorry for – for everything, and I'm really happy you got together."

"It was destiny," Bone joked. "If both our last names hadn't started with B, you might never have become my best friend. And if we hadn't become friends, I might never have met Hope." His voice and expression became suddenly serious. "And if you hadn't fallen for Bill..." He gave me a lopsided smile. "I guess things wouldn't have turned out as well as they did."

THAT'S THE WAY LOVE TURNED OUT FOR ME

Bill called me after Hope and Bone went home.

Even though I was still annoyed with him, my heart did a flip at the sound of his voice.

"I'm really sorry I didn't call you sooner, Michelle," he apologized, "but I've been busy all day." There was a sizzling sound. He was on the mobile.

"Wait'll you hear what happened," I said, trying to make myself heard over the shaky connection. "I thought Leonardo was dead."

Bill said, "Who?"

"Leonardo!" I was close to shouting. "My tortoise. You remember."

Bill laughed. "Of course I remember. The rock feet."

I didn't laugh. Bill wouldn't like it if I made a joke like that about his insane dog. "Rocks have no feelings," I said coolly. "Leonardo happens to be very sensitive." I was about to add "unlike you" when the line cut off for a nanosecond.

"What did you say happened to him?" Bill was asking.

"I thought he was dead," I screamed. "He wouldn't come out of his shell, and he hadn't moved all day—"

"What?" Bill shouted. "I'm sorry, Michelle, but the line's acting up. I can hardly hear you."

"He hadn't moved all day," I repeated, loudly, "and he smelled funny—"

"Did you say he was dead?" roared Bill.

"No, he's all right. Bone—"

"Look," Bill's voice crackled. "This is ridiculous. I wanted to know if you wanted to go to the cove tomorrow. For a barbecue. Layla and Hal are coming, too."

I hadn't meant to say anything, the words just came out. "I thought you went today. Your mother said—"

"No," Bill yelled. "Hal and I were just checking the new sail today."

A new sail! So they hadn't had their beach party without me! All the annoyance I'd been feeling melted away.

"Well, sure," I said quickly, as the connection wobbled again. "I'd love to go."

"Great," said Bill. "I'll pick you up at twelve."

* * *

That night I slept better than I had all week. I figured it was because everything was back to normal again with Bone and Hope and Bill. But I didn't dream about Bill, like I usually did. I dreamed that I was at a big party in the woods. There were silver balloons and flashing white Christmas lights strung through the trees. I was with Hope and Bone. Bill wasn't anywhere in sight. Bone had his guitar and Hope had her violin. They were playing "Louisiana Man" together, while I laid the party food out on my mother's old plaid car rug. My mother, John, Alfred Hitchcock, B.B. King, Leonardo the tortoise, Leonardo da Vinci, Che Guevara, and Mr Hunter were all there, too. B.B. King started playing along with Bone and Hope. Leonardo da Vinci was pumping Alfred Hitchcock for information on filmmaking. My mother and Mr Hunter were cracking each other up with jokes about Romeo and Juliet. Che Guevara and John were discussing motor cycles, and Leonardo was trying to get at the salad. He managed to get a leaf of lettuce stuck to his head. I picked him up and rubbed my nose against his. The last thing I put on the rug was an enormous chocolate cake with Leonardo written across the top and about a zillion lighted yellow candles on it. "Blow them all out!" everyone shouted. "Blow them all out!" I hadn't seen Bone and Hope put down their instruments, but suddenly they were beside me. Bone put his arms around our shoulders. "All together on the count of three," said Bone. "One… two … three…" We blew out the candles in a smoky cloud.

It was nearly eleven when I finally woke up. I stared at the clock for a few seconds, trying to remember why the time was important. Bill! He was taking me to the cove today. By the time I found something to wear, took a shower, and got dressed, it was nearly twelve. I raced into the kitchen for a glass of juice and a slice of toast before Bill arrived.

"Don't you look nice," said my mother as I flew past her. "I didn't realize this party was dress up."

I looked down at the slacks and silk shirt I'd put on – casual but sophisticated. "You don't think I look *too* dressed up, do you?" I asked. "I mean, it is on the beach."

John looked up from the paper he was reading. "On the beach? I thought we were having it here."

I stopped wondering if I should change into jeans. "What?" I asked. "What are you talking about?"

My mother smiled. "What are *you* talking about? John and I thought we were having a party for Leonardo today."

I went into shock. "Oh, no…" I moaned. Last night we'd all decided we really should celebrate Leonardo's survival. Bone called it an antiwake. "The party. I totally forgot!"

"If you hurry, you'll have time to get to the store for the food before Hope and Bone get here," said my mother. "One of us will drive you, won't we, John?"

"No problem," said John.

That was easy for him to say. I couldn't see anything *but* problems.

"We're going to have to have the party some other time," I said a little shrilly. "Bill's going to be here any minute to take me sailing."

My mother looked at John. John looked at the arts page.

"Well…" said my mother. "I guess it's no big deal…"

She was right. It wasn't a big deal. It was a casual last-minute thing. We could have the party Monday, after we took Leonardo to the vet. All I had to do was call Hope and explain what had happened.

The front bell rang. I ran from the room.

"Hurry up," said Bill as soon as I opened the door. "Hal and Layla are waiting at the dock."

I held open the door. "Come in for a second, I just have to make a quick phone call."

Bill rolled his eyes. "I know what a girl's idea of a quick phone call is."

"No, really. It'll just take a minute."

"I'll wait in the car," Bill decided. He

winked. "With the engine running. Don't be too long."

I rushed to the phone and called Hope.

"We were just about to leave," said Hope. "Bobby's brought all his B.B. King tapes to play for Leonardo and I bought him a bunch of watercress. Since it's a special occasion."

Well, it's not really that special, I answered her in my mind. *It's just a last-minute thing.*

A horn sounded outside.

Another voice in my mind answered me. *The barbecue isn't really special, either,* it said. *The barbecue is even more of a last-minute thing.* But the barbecue was with Bill and his friends. I'd promised I'd go. If I broke a date like this he really might never ask me out again.

I glanced towards the door. I could see Bill sitting in the jeep with a bored expression. I remembered my dream. And suddenly I knew why Bill hadn't been in my dream. Because he wouldn't have liked it. He wouldn't have fitted in.

"Give me half an hour," I said to Hope. "I have to go to the store or there'll be nothing for us to eat."

I wouldn't say that Bill's heart was broken by my change of plans.

"I could have been leaving the harbour by now," he grumbled. "Why didn't you tell me last night that you had something else to do?"

The funny thing was that my heart wasn't

broken, either. If anything I felt happier than I had for days. I was going to have a good afternoon.

"I told you," I said patiently. "I forgot."

"Yeah … well," said Bill. He put the jeep in reverse. "I've got to go, Michelle. I'll give you a call."

I didn't bother to ask when. "OK," I said. "Have a good time."

John waited in the car while I went into the supermarket. "Don't forget the tortilla chips," he called after me.

Clutching the list I'd written on the way, I raced into the store. I grabbed a cart, muttering, *"Tortilla chips … tortilla chips,"* under my breath. I grabbed a head of Leonardo's favourite lettuce as I steamed through Fruits and Vegetables.

I guess I wasn't paying attention again. One minute I was pushing my cart forward while I checked my list and the next there was this scream of pain. I looked up. It was like *déjà vu*. There, right in front of me, and more or less wedged between my cart and the tomatoes, was this guy. He looked really familiar. He was about eighteen, blond, not tall but very solid. He was just standing there, staring at me.

"I'm so sorry!" I apologized quickly, pulling the cart back a few centimetres. "I'm really, really sorry."

To my surprise, he started to laugh. "I don't believe it," he said, shaking his head. "It's you again." He had a really nice smile. "Have you been hired by enemy agents to run me over with your shopping cart, or is this just how you spend your spare time?"

I gazed back at him in horror. He was wearing a blue flannel shirt under his denim jacket this time, but it was the same guy I'd ploughed into the last time I'd been in the supermarket, with Hope. "Oh, my God," I gasped. "I really am sorry. I didn't do it on purpose... I'm in a hurry and I wasn't looking where I was going and—"

He cut me off. "Wait, a minute, you're not an enemy agent. I know you, don't I?"

"No," I said, shaking my head. "No, I don't think—"

He snapped his fingers, pointing to the lettuce in my cart. "Tortoise," he said. "You own a spur-thighed tortoise." He screwed up his eyes for a second, like he was thinking, then he snapped his fingers again. "Leonardo," he said. He smiled. "After da Vinci."

I was so surprised I could hardly speak. "What are you, psychic or something?" I managed to say.

He stuck out his hand. "My name's Jack. Jack Abrams." He smiled again. It was a nice smile.

I took his hand automatically. "Abrams?"

238

For the first time I really looked at him. "Abrams!" I repeated. And then I remembered. I hadn't seen him for a couple of years, but he used to help out at the vet's in the summer. "You're Dr Abrams' son."

"That's right," he said, laughing. "We used to talk about reptiles, remember?"

I laughed, too. "Mona!" I said. "You have an iguana named Mona!"

"That's right." He really did have a nice smile. "But I can't remember your name."

"Mike," I said, suddenly aware that he was still holding my hand. "Mike Brindisi."

"So, Mike Brindisi," said Jack. "Do you think if I bought you a coffee sometime when you're not in a hurry, you might stop trying to mow me down?"

His brown eyes had tiny flecks of gold in them. "Well," I stumbled, "I…"

"Oh, come on," said Jack. "We can't keep meeting like this. I'll be crippled before we have our first date."

And that's how I met the boy of my dreams.

CONFESSIONS OF A
TEENAGE DRAMA QUEEN

Dyan Sheldon

Everything I'm about to tell you occurred exactly as I say. And I don't just mean the stuff about "Deadwood" High, and my fight with Carla Santini over the school play. I mean everything. Even the things that seem so totally out of this solar system that you think I must have made them up – like crashing the party after Sidartha's farewell concert in New York – they're true too. And nothing's been exaggerated. Not the teeniest, most sub-atomic bit. It all happened exactly as I'm telling it.

And it starts with the end of the world...

"An outrageously funny and fast-moving story."
The Northern Echo

"Delicious reading... Home-grown drama queens and teen shrinking violets will love it." *Kids Out*

AND BABY MAKES TWO

Dyan Sheldon

"Happiness was mine. This was what I'd always wanted. Plus, having a baby beat taking my GCSEs."

Lana Spiggs is fed up with everyone telling her what to do – her mother, her teachers... What Lana wants is to be grown up, with her own flat, her own husband and her own children – and no one will be able to boss her around any more.

Then on her fifteenth birthday, Lana meets Les. She knows he's the one and when she gets pregnant, it seems that her wishes are about to come true at last. But can Lana's dream of Happy Families stand up to reality?

By turns funny and hard-hitting, this tale of a teenage mother is a compelling read.

TALL, THIN AND BLONDE

Dyan Sheldon

Torn between the weird and the glamorous, which way will Jenny go?

Best friends Jenny and Amy have no time for Miss Perfect Teenagers, the tall, thin blondes whose only talk is of boys and fashion. At least they didn't. Now, suddenly Amy's changed: she's into salads and diet Cokes; she's got a new hairstyle, wardrobe and set of friends. Jenny, meanwhile, finds herself part of a group of oddballs nicknamed the Martians. Will she follow Amy or find her own way?

"The teenage girl's lot ... is treated with empathy and humour." *The Times Educational Supplement*

"Frequently hilarious." *The Irish Times*

RIDE ON, SISTER VINCENT

Dyan Sheldon

"A miracle. That's what St Agnes really needs. A miracle, not a motor mechanic."

Sent to the dilapidated convent school, St Agnes in the Pasture, dynamic, globe-trotting Sister Vincent, teacher of motor mechanics, feels like a fish out of water. Certainly Mother Margaret Aloysius, the nuns and the school's three young pupils consider her a bit of an odd fish. The Lord, it seems, is moving in a very mysterious way indeed – until a discovery in the old barn enables Sister Vincent to give the run-down school a surprising and exhilarating kick-start!

THE BOY-FREE ZONE

Veronica Bennett

What's the use of being the best-looking girl in town when there are no boys to notice you?

Living in the Boy-free Zone of Broughton, fifteen-year-old Annabel "Barbie-Brain" Bairstow is facing the long summer holiday without enthusiasm. Then Sebastian appears... Seventeen years old, handsome, self-confident *and* American, Sebastian has the impact of a bombshell on Annabel and her friends. Already trying to come to terms with her parents' divorce, Annabel finds herself confronted by some alarming surprises. Most surprising of all, though, is the discovery of the power that lies in her own hands...

Enter the Boy-free Zone for a story full of intrigue and passion, by the author of the acclaimed *Monkey*.

THE LIFE AND LOVES OF ZOË T. CURLEY

Martin Waddell

It's not easy being an aspiring teenager with a brace and the body of a "fat elephant".

This is the lot of Zoë T. Curley, prisoner of Zog, the life-system invented by Zoë's temperamental writer father to keep order in the Curley household. Fortunately Zoë has a loyal best friend, Melissa, with whom she can discuss her many domestic woes, as well as such vital matters as BOYS and LOVE. Follow Zoë's fluctuating fortunes throughout one turbulent month in this entertaining diary novel.

"Acutely observed." *The Daily Mail*

TANGO'S BABY

Martin Waddell

Tango is not one of life's romantic heroes.

Even his few friends are amazed to learn of his love affair with young Crystal O'Leary, the girl he fancies and who seemed to have no interest in him. Next thing they know, she's pregnant – and that's when the real story of Tango's baby begins. By turns tragic and farcical, it's a story in which many claim a part, but few are able to help Tango as he strives desperately to keep his new family together.

"Waddell is as ever an excellent storyteller."
The Independent

"Brilliantly written." *The Sunday Telegraph*

SECOND STAR TO THE RIGHT

Deborah Hautzig

I wouldn't be half bad-looking if I were thin. 5'5½", blue eyes, long light brown hair, small hips – and 125 pounds. If I were thin, my life would be perfect.

On the face of it, Leslie is a normal, healthy, well-adjusted fourteen-year-old girl. She goes to a good school, has a great friend in Cavett, and a mother who loves her to the moon and back. She should be happy, yet she's not. She would be, if only she were thinner. But how thin do you have to be to find happiness?

This is a haunting, honest, utterly compelling account of a girl in the grip of anorexia nervosa.